Grimmtastic Girls

Rapunzel Cuts Loose

Grimmtastic Girls

Grimmtastic Girls

Rapunzel Cuts Loose

Joan Holub & Suzanne Williams

Scholastic Inc.

No part of this publication may be reproduced, stored in a retrieval system, or transmitted in any form or by any means, electronic, mechanical, photocopying, recording, or otherwise, without written permission of the publisher. For information regarding permission, write to Scholastic Inc., Attention: Permissions Department, 557 Broadway, New York, NY 10012.

ISBN 978-0-545-51986-1

Text copyright © 2014 by Joan Holub and Suzanne Williams
All rights reserved. Published by Scholastic Inc.
SCHOLASTIC and associated logos are trademarks and/or registered trademarks of Scholastic Inc.

12 11 10 9 8 7 6 5 4 3 2 1   14 15 16 17 18 19/0

Printed in the U.S.A.   40
First printing, October 2014
Designed by Yaffa Jaskoll

For our grimmazing readers:

Megan D., Micci S., The Andrade Family, Alba C., Mona P.,
Emily M., Lana W., Tawney K., Yesenia O., Meghan B.,
Rianne R., Emily B., Amber T., Lori F., Caitlin R., Micaila S.,
McKay O., Reese O., Kierra C., Leyi S., Leslie S., Caitlynn L.,
Angelina D., Vivian Z., Stacy J., Ally M., Angela C.,
Sabrina C., Shelly B., Christine D-H., Khanya S., Thea F-S.,
Shannon Y., Andrea C., Josephine W., Angelina D., Jolee S.,
Jenna S., Sarah S., Kristen H., Julie H., Paul H., and you!

And a huge Grimmstone Library size thank you to
Amanda M. and Sarah E.

— JH and SW

Contents

It is written upon the wall of the great Grimmstone Library:

Something E.V.I.L. this way comes.
To protect all that is born of fairy tale, folktale, and nursery
rhyme magic, we have created the realm of Grimmlandia. In
the center of this realm, we have built two castles on opposite
ends of a Great Hall, which straddles the Once Upon River. And
this haven shall be forever known as Grimm Academy.

~ The brothers Grimm

1

The Message

Rapunzel lifted the silver chain that hung around her neck, and poked the key that dangled from it into the lock on her trunker — a fancy leather trunk that stood tallwise on its end like a locker among other trunkers lining the school hallway. As she turned the key, she softly sang her unlocking combination. *"I love to dance, dilly dilly, I love to sing. When I am queen, dilly dilly, you'll be my king."*

Most of the unlocking combinations at Grimm Academy were short and could be chanted or spoken, but she'd gotten a long one, and it had to be sung in tune. Luckily, she had a good voice.

"Hey! Thanks for the offer. But I'm too young to get married," a boy called out. It was Basil von Valerian. As he went to his trunker nearby, Rapunzel sent him a quick glance, her lips curling into a smile. He was a head taller than she was, with light brown hair and mischievous green eyes full of good humor.

Rapunzel's three best friends here at school were girls — Snow White, Red Riding Hood, and Cinderella. But Basil was her guy BFF. They'd been friends ever since she'd rescued him from a bully named Little Jack Horner on the first day of first grade. Jack had been such a bully that teachers had often made him sit in a corner where he couldn't bother other students.

"Ha-ha," she said to Basil as her trunker door swung open. "We're only twelve. Besides, I'm not a princess and you're not a prince. So how could I ever make you a king or —" Rapunzel's tongue froze as she noticed the boy opening the trunker just beyond Basil. Prince Perfect. Her super-secret crush.

He was the only boy in school who could make her blush with embarrassment over nothing and stumble over her words. Seeing him unsettled her, and her hand trembled as she reached for her Academy Handbook. As she pulled it from its shelf, a mouse-shaped cat toy tumbled out of her trunker and rolled halfway across the hall. *Tink, tink, tink* went its bell.

"Oh, frogwoggle," she murmured under her breath. There was a flash of blue in her long glossy black hair as she flipped it over one shoulder and scurried after the toy. She grabbed it, then quickly ran back and stuck it in her trunker.

She'd worn her hair mostly loose today, with only the

blue-streaked sections woven into a series of intricate braids at the back of her head. Some people thought the blue strands were dyed, but they were actually natural. Good thing, because her hair grew a foot or longer every single day, which meant she would've had to re-dye the streaks daily to keep up. Sometimes her hair grew inches in just minutes. She had cut it to waist length yesterday morning, but already it hung down to her knees. By nightfall it would touch the floor.

Realizing that both boys were staring at her now, she explained lamely, "That silly nursery rhyme I was singing is just my trunker combination. The one Ms. Jabberwocky gave me at the beginning of school." She was babbling like an idiot. *Stop it!* she told herself.

Basil shot her a weird look as he shut his trunker door with the nudge of an elbow. "Duh, yeah, I know that obviously. I've only heard you sing it about a million times. It was a joke, Rapunzel."

"Oh. Yeah. A joke," she echoed. She'd known that. But Prince Perfect might not have. She'd really only said all that for his benefit. She didn't want him to think Basil was her crush or anything. Unfortunately, she'd wound up sounding kind of bubbleheaded.

She dug aimlessly around in her trunker, rearranging the row of dark nail polishes on the top shelf in rainbow order, starting with Redtabulous and ending with Velvet

Violet. But her attention was fixed on Perfect, and she kept giving him sidelong glances. There were so many princes going to GA that they all just went by their last names. And the name Perfect fit him *perfectly*, in her opinion. Tall with dark hair, he wasn't just cute like most boys at the Academy. He was *handsome*, like the princes in the great fairy-tale books penned by Wilhelm and Jacob Grimm.

"Hey, Rapunzel! Want to meet in the dungeon after school to talk about . . . stuff?" called Cinderella, who went by Cinda for short. Her trunker was directly across the hall, with Snow and Red Riding Hood's on either side of it. Those three Grimm girls were all looking Rapunzel's way now, the same question in their eyes.

"Stuff? Sounds intriguing," said Prince Awesome, whose trunker was two down from Prince Perfect's. He wiggled his eyebrows at Cinda, his crush, and she grinned back.

Rapunzel knew what *stuff* her friends wanted to discuss. Secret stuff. Like treasure! And how to find it. At Prince Awesome's ball a few weeks ago, they'd accidentally discovered a mapestry, which was currently hidden in the cute nut-brown wicker basket Red held over one arm. It was a magical map in the form of a stitched tapestry that showed the entire realm of Grimmlandia, including the Academy. They hoped it would lead to a legendary treasure so enormously valuable that it would save the school from financial ruin at the hands of a terrible secret society. A society called E.V.I.L. (as in *E*xceptional *V*illains *I*n *L*iterature).

"Okay. Sounds good," Rapunzel told her friends in answer to Cinda's question.

Prince Perfect gave her a sideways glance. She really wished he hadn't overheard Cinda's mention of the dungeon. Rapunzel didn't like calling attention to the fact that she was . . . different. That while all the other girls lived in the three tower dorms on the fifth and sixth floors of the Academy, she chose to live deep down in the school's dungeon.

Bong! The sound of the huge Hickory Dickory Dock grandfather clock over in the Great Hall echoed throughout the school, signaling the hour. Everyone who was dawdling in the hallway or at a trunker suddenly shot off in different directions, all heading to their third-period classes.

Snow, Cinda, and Red quickly murmured their trunker locking combinations. They looked like a pretty bouquet of girl-size flowers in their colorful dresses. Only Rapunzel was wearing all black — ankle boots, leggings, dress, bag. Everything. As usual. It was her favorite color, as everyone knew.

Snow's dress was turquoise. It was a color she'd been wearing a lot lately — ever since she'd found a certain sparkly tiara with turquoise jewels in it. Cinda wore pink, which looked grimmazing with her long candle-flame yellow hair and blue eyes. She was on the masketball team sixth period and often wore pink-laced sneakers. But today, she had on her glass slippers.

Red carried her basket of course, and the dress and hooded cape she wore matched the red streaks in her dark, curly hair. Her basket could fetch things if asked in just the right manner. However, it would obey only Red. Because it was her magical charm — which was far more important and not at all the same thing as a lucky charm.

Snow's tiara was *her* magical charm. Cinda had a magical charm, too — her glass slippers. In fact, of the four Grimm girls, Rapunzel was the only one who hadn't yet received her charm. Which was okay, really. Most students went to the Academy for *ages* before their special charms appeared. Still, it would be nice to have one!

The three girls waved farewell to Rapunzel as they dashed off to their classes in a whirl of satin and silk, each carrying their Academy Handbooks. She hurriedly crooned the relocking half of her combination. *"Who told you so, dilly dilly, who told you so? 'Twas my own heart, dilly dilly, that told me so,"* she sang softly. It was a beautiful song, but a bit *silly silly*, if you asked her.

Her trunker lock snapped into place and she slipped her key out of the lock. Instantly, an image of her face magically painted itself in the small heart-shaped inset on the trunker, right above the lock. Dark almond-shaped eyes, and lips glossed a red that was so deep the color looked almost black.

She tucked her Handbook under one arm. Lifting the hem of her long black skirt with her free hand, she sprinted down the first-floor hall of Pink Castle. The marble walls here were a pretty pale pink and were hung with tapestries showing scenes of feasts and pageantry.

Rounding one of the tall stone support columns, whose top was carved with figures of birds, flowers, and gargoyles, her eyes went to the magnificent grand staircase in the school entrance. She could see Basil, Perfect, and Awesome up ahead of her. Most classes on this side of the school were all-girl, but some included boys. And all three of these boys were in her third-period Bespellings and Enchantments class.

When Basil dropped back to walk with her, Rapunzel shot him a grateful half smile. He knew she was deathly afraid of heights and hated stairs. In fact, she rarely climbed to the dorms, or even higher than the third floor. Taking a deep breath, she started up the steps with him. "How's everything coming for the festival this weekend?" he asked, probably hoping to distract her before she could get nervous. Too late!

"Pretty good," she replied. "That's some of the *stuff* Cinda and the others probably want to talk about after school." Rapunzel and her three BFFs had come up with the idea of a festival as a way to earn money to boost the Academy's finances while they continued to look for treasure. It was Thursday and they'd be discussing last-minute plans and divvying up final chores to do because the festival began the day after tomorrow!

"Well, tell them that the guys — Awesome, Foulsmell, Perfect, Prince, and me — are working on a last-minute game for the festival. Wait till you see." The first three princes he named were in their next-period class. The last one was actually named Prince Prince, his first and last names being the same.

They'd reached the second-floor landing. Only one more floor to go. Rapunzel's fingers gripped the handrail tighter the higher they went. "So what is it? Your amazing thing for the festival?" she asked, trying to keep her mind off her fears.

"Not telling yet. It's a surprise."

Rapunzel glanced over to see him grinning. Then her eyes flicked ahead. *Just ten more steps.* She gritted her teeth.

"So, are you going to the Festival Ball Sunday night?" Basil asked a few seconds later.

"Mmm-hmm. With my friends," Rapunzel replied, her mind on each step they took upward. *Two more left.* "You?"

At last! They'd reached the point where the grand staircase split off into smaller twisty stairs that went higher and higher. But they weren't going up farther, thank goodness!

"So I was wondering . . ." Basil began. Leaning against the door to the third floor, he pushed it open with one shoulder, and they stepped out into the hall. Rapunzel was just breathing a huge sigh of relief to be done with all those stairs, when suddenly, a ball of black fur whipped by, crossing right in front of her.

"Whoa!" She tripped, falling forward and tumbling to her knees. Her long hair spilled around her in a tangle of glossy black. The cat she'd just tripped over scampered up to her and licked her cheek in a friendly way. He obviously had no idea he had almost caused a dangerous accident.

"Mordred!" scolded Rapunzel, sitting back to glare at him. "How did you get here so fast, you bad boy? I just left you in the dun — uh, my room, not ten minutes ago." He was one of her five cats, a black one with a white star on his forehead. The only one who seemed to halfway understand her when she talked to him. When he felt like listening, that is.

"Hey, you okay?" Basil reached out to help her up.

Feeling embarrassed, she shrugged his hand away. "Yes," she snapped, jumping to her feet on her own.

Basil reared back with his palms out, pretending he was shielding himself from her mood. "Overreact much?" he asked in a teasing tone.

"Sorry," she said sheepishly. "I guess I get kind of grumpy when my own cat practically tries to kill me."

She pushed her hair back over a shoulder and glanced ahead. Perfect was way down the hall now. Unfortunately, he was looking back at her and she was sure he'd witnessed her fall.

"Yeah, what's up with you, crazy cat?" asked Basil. As he bent down to pick up Rapunzel's Handbook for her, he gave the cat a quick pat, ruffling its fur. A puff of white poofed up into the air.

"Mordred, what have you been up to?" Rapunzel asked the cat, who appeared to be covered with a light dusting of white powder. She picked him up and gave him a quick dust-off, causing both Basil and her to sneeze. *Achoo! Achoo!*

She sniffed the cat's head. "Flour and a hint of cinnamon," she announced.

"Was he down in the Great Hall kitchen?" Basil wondered.

Rapunzel's eyes narrowed and she went still as she caught sight of the small crystal orb tied to Mordred's collar. It was a message marble! Such marbles usually contained important time-sensitive information from their senders. This one had clearly been sent by Mistress

Hagscorch. For one thing, it had her initials carved on it. A dead giveaway. She was the cook and head of the school cafeteria down on the first floor. Also one of the scariest grown-ups at the Academy.

"More likely in the Pearl Tower dorm," answered Rapunzel. "Red's tower task is Snackmaker, remember? She bakes cookies up there all the time." Actually, she was pretty sure Basil was correct about where the cat had been, but she had her reasons for not wanting him to know he'd guessed right.

She reached for the marble, but before she could even touch it, Mordred leaped from her arms. "Here, kitty," she called sweetly. But Mordred sauntered off down the hall as if he hadn't heard her. She took off after him, but he quickened his pace to keep just out of reach. "Come on. Come here, and I'll ... take you to the festival this weekend, okay?" she offered.

The cat paused and turned his head to look at her. He twitched his tail and almost seemed to grin at her in a satisfied way. Then, with one enormous leap, he bounded into her arms.

"Not a bad bargain," said Basil, as he caught up with her outside the classroom door. Then he added, "For the *cat*."

"What do you mean?"

"I mean that you're a pushover." He gave Mordred's head a gentle stroke and the cat purred.

"Am not!" Rapunzel protested.

"Face it. You couldn't bargain your way out of a paper bag," he said with a grin. "At least when it comes to cats."

Meowww!

"Oh, sorry, Mordred!" In her consternation, she'd hugged him a little too hard without realizing it. Now she nuzzled the top of his head with her chin. Except for one bad deal she'd made when she was only six, she didn't think she totally stunk at deal making. Oh, wait a minute — there was also that bad bargain she'd made with Hagscorch earlier this year. *Hmm. Maybe I* am *a pushover.*

She hoped not! That was the very last thing she wanted to be. Her parents had been pretty much the worst deal makers ever in the history of Grimmlandia and she'd promised herself not to be like them. Why, before she was even born, they'd bargained her away to a witch!

2

Tongue Twisters

"C'mon, we're late," Rapunzel told Basil. She set her cat down in the hall. At the same time, she stealthily pulled off the crystal marble tied to his collar, making sure Basil didn't see. The reason Hagscorch regularly contacted her was something Rapunzel kept a secret from everyone, including her best friends. Anyway, the grumpy cook had already sent her instructions for the week. *So why this new, additional message?* she wondered nervously.

Although anxious to read it, Rapunzel stood up and tucked the marble into her pocket with a smooth gesture. Turning, she led the way into Bespellings and Enchantments class. She would read the message privately, as soon as she could.

Feeling something brush her ankle boots, she looked down to see that Mordred had followed her into the room. Cats were allowed in some classes, including this one. Still, since they'd be casting spells this period, it might be dangerous. She didn't want anyone to accidentally turn Mordred into a toad. Or something worse!

She leaned down, stared her cat straight in his green eyes, and wagged a finger in his face. "Back to the dungeon with you or our deal's off, okay?" she warned. "Scoot."

Mordred blinked at her. Then he rubbed his cheek against her hand. *Mrrr.* Which meant *affirmative* in Mordred-speak — but she didn't trust that cat one bit. He was a wanderer, always getting into mischief. If he was cooped up in her room while she was gone, he'd chew up all of her belongings. So she always left the high dungeon window open for him to come and go.

As the cat hightailed it out of the classroom, Rapunzel took her seat at one of the three long tables. They were lined up, one behind another, facing the teacher's desk at the front of the room. Rapunzel's table was in the middle and Basil and his princely friends, Perfect, Awesome, and Foulsmell, were seated at the far end of it.

"A magical good morning to you all, class!" trilled Ms. Blue Fairygodmother. She tapped her wand on her desk, and then stood. A huge bubble of pale blue light surrounded her. Instead of walking, she floated inside her bubble to stand before her desk, hovering a few inches above the ground. Freaky. But in a grimmarkable sort of way!

With everyone's attention on her, Ms. Blue said, "Open your Handbooks to Chapter Nine, please."

Realizing that Basil still had her book, Rapunzel leaned out and motioned for him to pass it to her, which he did.

"Crush alert!" Prince Foulsmell teased. He put his hand over his heart and patted it really fast, to imply that Basil's heart was racing just because she was nearby.

Awesome and Perfect stared hard at Basil as if trying to figure out if this were true.

As if, thought Rapunzel, rolling her eyes. They were pals, that's all. She hoped Prince Perfect knew that.

Rapunzel pressed a fingertip to the raised oval shape on her Handbook's cover. There was a swirly gold-stamped *GA* (for Grimm Academy, of course) logo inside the oval. All school subjects were contained in one Handbook, but not all at once. Students had to ask for whatever subject they wanted for it to appear.

"Bespellings and Enchantments," she instructed her book. Then she opened it to find that the first page was printed with the words:

This
Grimm Academy
Handbook
belongs to
Rapunzel.

Third period:

Bespellings and Enchantments

Rapunzel thumbed down the contents page and pressed her fingertip over the words *Chapter Nine: Enchanted Plants*. Her book magically flipped its pages open to the chapter she'd chosen. There, she found pictures of weird plants such as talking cacti and strange-looking strangler vines. She tapped one of the pictures. Up popped a lifelike Venus flytrap. It snapped at her nose, making her jump back in surprise. Then it snapped back into the book, becoming a flat picture on the page again.

"Today we will grow tongue twisters," Ms. Blue announced to the class. Every eye followed her as she floated back and forth at the front of the room. "Tongue twisters are phrases or sentences that are difficult to speak quickly. Can anyone tell me why that might be?"

Mary Mary Quite Contrary, the red-haired girl who was seated on Rapunzel's left, waved her hand high. When called on, she summarized the words from the first page in Chapter Nine, saying, "Because they contain repeated sequences of words with very, very similar sounds."

"Precisely." Ms. Blue Fairygodmother gave her wand a brisk wave in the air, making a musical trill. *Schwing!* Twenty terra-cotta flowerpots magically appeared on the tabletops, one before each student. Rapunzel tilted hers to look inside. It was empty. She waited for Ms. Blue to explain the purpose of the pots, but instead, the teacher asked, "Now, can anyone tell us the value of tongue twisters?"

"Actors use them," Rapunzel volunteered when no one else said anything. She'd heard Red Riding Hood and her crush, Wolfgang, speaking tongue twisters before their Drama class. "To sort of loosen up, in preparation for reading lines of dialogue."

Ms. Blue nodded approvingly. "Yes, tongue twisters can certainly help develop speech skills. They even play an occasional part in some of the nursery rhymes preserved here in Grimmlandia by the Grimm brothers. Besides that, they're fun to try to say."

Her musical laughter rang out as she waved her wand again. "I have just magically placed a seed packet inside your pot. Please use the letter inside it to create the words you will speak aloud in order to grow your tongue twister. Remember that you must only speak the words of your tongue twister directly to your pot. We don't want to grow twisters on one another!"

Everyone chuckled over that and then began opening their packets. Everyone except Rapunzel. Normally, she loved this class, with its vials of bubbling potions and shelves of weird objects that wriggled, whispered, and sometimes let out screeches or squeaks. She could study for a thousand years and never learn everything there was to know about magic!

But today, her mind was on that message marble and what instructions it might contain. In the general noisy shuffle of students getting to work, she pulled the small, round crystal from her pocket.

She leaned forward, letting her long hair drape like a curtain around her so the girls on either side of her wouldn't see what she did next. Opening her hand in her lap, she gazed at the clear marble in her palm and waited for the message to reveal itself. It didn't take long. Within seconds, the marble dissolved and expanded into a ball of pale gray mist as big as her palm. Black letters formed in the mist, running across it in a line. Quickly she read them before they could disappear for good. It wasn't hard, because this particular message contained only one word repeated over and over: *Rampion. Rampion. Rampion.*

Rapunzel stared at the words, feeling the blood drain from her face. When she finished reading, the mist gathered itself smaller and turned to a solid crystal marble again. Mistress Hagscorch's initials were gone from the marble now, so that it could be reused by anyone. She tucked it into her black bag and pushed her hair back over her shoulders.

Mary Mary looked over just then. She stared hard at Rapunzel's face. "What's wrong? What's wrong? Are you sick?" the girl demanded in alarm. She jerked her head back as if afraid of catching germs. "You look like you feel really, really terrible. Like maybe . . . like maybe you just saw a *ghost flower*!"

"Is a ghost flower a plant that actually grows in the Bouquet Garden?" a princess named Pea asked from the table behind theirs.

Mary Mary shook her head. "No! To see one causes a fever that makes you go pale." *She would be the one to know*, thought Rapunzel. Her tower task was Gardenkeeper, which meant she was in charge of the big garden that grew on the grounds surrounding Grimm Academy.

At the beginning of every school year, a tower task was assigned to each student for the entire term. Putting Mary Mary in charge of the garden had seemed an odd match to Rapunzel. Flowers were so bright and cheery and, well, *agreeable*. Yet Mary Mary Quite Contrary was positively *negative* about pretty much everything.

This year, Cinda had gotten the task of Hearthkeeper, Snow was Tidy-upper, and Red Riding Hood was Snackmaker. But Rapunzel had kept her task a secret from everyone. Because it was way grimmbarrassing. She'd been chosen as a Gatherer, a task usually assigned just to witches! And that was something Rapunzel did not want anyone thinking she would grow up to be. Yet in the depths of her heart, she feared it could happen one day.

As a Gatherer, her job was to help gather whatever Mistress Hagscorch needed in the way of herbs, spices, and hard-to-find veggies once a week. The cook used them to concoct the rather strange, but tasty, meals she served each day in the Academy's Great Hall.

"Know what I think?" asked Mary Mary. Then, without waiting for an answer, she went on. "You should go, go, *go* see the doctor, the nurse, and that lady with the alligator purse in the infirmary." She flicked her fingers toward the door, shooing Rapunzel away.

"I'm okay," she insisted before Mary Mary could start everyone worrying that she'd caught something contagious, which she hadn't. But Mary Mary was right about one thing. Rapunzel did feel kind of like she'd just seen a ghost. One from her past that wore a pointy black hat. She shivered.

Why had Mistress Hagscorch requested rampion? She never had before. Rampion was a magical, spinachlike plant that grew in only one location in Grimmlandia as far as Rapunzel knew — the deep, dark, very scary Neverwood Forest. The woods where everyone said you "never would" go if you had half a brain. The rampion patch grew there, at the foot of a tower that was guarded by a witch. The very witch who'd raised her until she was six years old! And Rapunzel was not going back to see her. Nuh-uh. No way. She'd have to talk Hagscorch out of this assignment. But how?

She snapped back to attention when Ms. Blue clapped her hands together in delight. "I almost forgot the most exciting part of this assignment," said the teacher. "Your tongue twister pot plants will be used to help decorate the grounds on Heart Island for the Grimmlandia Festival this weekend. Festival attendees will judge your creations, and awards will be given to the top three." She paused before adding, "The awards will include no-homework days and tokens for free items in The Cupboard."

At this, Foulsmell punched a fist in the air. "Yes!" Basil and Awesome high-fived as excited murmurs filled the room. The Cupboard was a small supply store on the fourth floor of the Academy, run by a shopkeeper named Old Mother Hubbard. It was stocked with regular stuff like vellum paper and quill pens, but also with oddball curiosities such as magical bones.

"I heard it was going to rain on Saturday," Mary Mary informed everyone within earshot. Rapunzel rolled her eyes. Leave it to Mary Mary to be a wet blanket.

When Ms. Blue began floating around the room in her ball of light to check on students' progress, Rapunzel realized she'd better get busy. She checked inside her pot and found a small packet. After tearing it open, she discovered within it a single seed that was shaped like the letter *W*. But what was she supposed to do with it exactly? She skimmed the chapter that gave directions.

Create a tongue twister in which more than half of the words begin with the sound of your assigned letter or letter group, she read silently. Immediately, *W* words began to fill her mind, and she wrote various combinations of them on a blank sheet of vellum. *Wand, wish, walrus, wonky . . . witch*. No! She scratched out that last one.

It was no secret at GA that she'd been raised by a witch (it was written in the Grimm tales, after all), but she was *not* a witch herself and she would *never* become one. Not if she could help it!

All around her, others began chanting tongue twisters at their flowerpots. Spirits were high and there was much giggling.

One table up, Goldilocks leaned toward her flowerpot and chanted loudly: "Five fuzzy bears followed four furry foxes in the forest." Obviously she'd gotten the seed letter *F*. There were gasps all around as a leafy green vine sprang from the soil in her pot and coiled upward. Nine blossoms instantly opened to reveal five little stuffed fuzzy bears and four furry toy foxes. Adorable!

The teacher paused to admire the plant, then instructed Goldilocks to go further. "To get even more blossoms, repeat your tongue twister quickly over and over, as many times as you can, without stumbling or mispronouncing. The more times you say your twister correctly, the more objects will blossom."

"And that will increase your chances of making a plant that wins an award at the festival!" Rapunzel heard a bubbly voice say. It was Mermily, who sat on her other side. She was a mermaid and Cinda's roommate in Pearl Tower dorm.

Now Mermily chanted a tongue twister into her flowerpot: "Shy Shari Shellfish sells shiny seashells to ships by the seashore." She managed to say it three times without a mistake. A vine with three large, shiny seashells curled upward from the soil in her pot.

Rapunzel looked over to see that Mermily had gotten a seed in the shape of the letter group *SH*. "Nice job," she told her.

Mary Mary let out a big sigh. "I absolutely hate, hate, *hate* my letter," she complained when Rapunzel looked her way. "Will you trade?"

"Sure," Rapunzel agreed, knowing that Mary Mary would probably have complained no matter what letter she got. And would keep on complaining until someone traded with her. She handed off her *W*, then looked at the letter Mary passed to her in exchange. An *X*? What was she going to do with that? It really *was* an awful choice to get stuck with. Without thinking, she'd made a truly stinky bargain! She frowned at Mary Mary.

"A deal's a deal," Mary Mary said quickly. "No givebacks."

Down the table, the boys started joking around. "I got the letter *B*," Perfect announced. "Hmm . . . Basil starts with a *B*. . . ." He paused then, appearing totally stumped about how to go on.

Mary Mary eyed him dreamily. When Ms. Blue wasn't looking, she scribbled something on a slip of paper, which she then folded and held high in her hand. Instantly, a blue bird swooped in from the open window and carried her note to Perfect.

He read the note, and then smiled at her. Holding it before him, he chanted aloud to his pot. "Basil bought a big beautiful blossoming bouquet of bright blue begonias . . . with boogers." *Whoosh!* A vine shot up and a bouquet of blue flowers speckled with boogers blossomed forth.

All of the guys around Perfect cracked up.

"Eew!" said Mermily. She and Rapunzel frowned at Mary Mary.

Mary Mary's eyes widened. "I did not, not, *not* write the booger part," she assured them. "Perfect added that himself."

"Way to get a girl to do your work for you," Foulsmell told the prince wryly. In fact, Rapunzel thought, girls often *did* do things for Perfect. It wasn't really fair or right, but something about him — his perfect looks, perhaps — just made every girl want to do whatever it took to get his attention.

"My turn," Basil said. "It so happens I got *P*." After giving Perfect a mock-evil grin, he stared at his pot.

Then he came up with a doozy of a chant. "Prince Perfect picked a perfect peck of purple pickles. A peck of purple pickles Prince Perfect perfectly picked. If Prince Perfect picked a perfect peck of purple pickles, where's the peck of purple pickles Prince Perfect perfectly picked?" He managed to repeat all of that five times without a mistake.

Everyone laughed as a vine hanging with bunches of purple pickles whooshed up from Basil's pot. Perfect reached out and snatched off one of the bunches.

"Hey!" complained Basil.

"Sorry!" said Perfect. "But your twister did say I picked them." Which was kind of funny, thought Rapunzel. But still, Perfect shouldn't have done that. Now there was a blank spot on Basil's plant.

However, the easygoing Basil fixed this by simply repeating his tongue twister, which caused the empty spot to fill in. Rapunzel quit watching the boys so she could attend to her own troublesome tongue twister.

She racked her brain for *X* words. *Ibex, hex, ox, ax, fox, pixie.* But she couldn't use them. Her words had to *start* with *X.* Oh, wait! Maybe *xylophone* would work. She practically gave herself a headache trying to think up any more *X* words, though. Then she remembered that their book said the words in tongue twisters must begin with similar *sounds*, not necessarily *letters. Hmm.* Since the *X* in *xylophone* sounded like *Z*, could she use *Z* words, too? That would give her more choices. She wrote some ideas, finally ending up with: "Zany Zachary zigzagged alone through the zoo's zebra zone with his xylophone." She said it four times without making a mistake.

Up whooshed a vine. Immediately, eight-inch-long xylophones and little toy zebras bloomed upon it. Delighted, she pulled out her pen and tapped out a little tune on the colored bars of one of the xylophones, which made the students around her laugh.

"No! No fair. You only used one *X* — *one X* — in your whole twister," Mary Mary was swift to point out.

"But it rhymed," Mermily noted. "So actually I think you should get extra points!" she told Rapunzel.

"Thanks," Rapunzel replied, smiling. Then she turned to Mary Mary. "Need any help with yours?" she asked, hoping her offer would keep the girl from calling more attention to her own possible bending of the rules.

Mary Mary sighed deeply and leaned over to show her the words she'd come up with. "I want to write a twister with the word *wiggle* in it. Only I can't think of anything good."

Rapunzel suggested a few rearrangements of the words on Mary Mary's list. Then the girl began, saying, "If a wacky wiggly white worm . . ."

Just then, something soft and slinky wound around Rapunzel's ankles. She looked down. "Mordred!" He hadn't left the classroom after all, that bad cat! The cat ignored her, eyeing Mary Mary with a rascally expression. *Uh-oh!* He loved chasing anything wiggly — including worms!

". . . waved at a wig-wearing wiggling worm whizzing by," Mary Mary went on, "which worm would be the . . ." Rapunzel leaned down to grab Mordred, but he leaped past her and up onto the table. Standing right in front of Mary Mary, he shook himself. Enough flour dust was left in his fur to poof into the air, causing her to stutter and then sneeze out the final word of her chant. ". . . wig . . . uh . . . wig . . . *wiggliest*?"

Rapunzel managed to turn away just in time, so the sneeze didn't hit her in the face. Instead, it only went into her hair.

"Oh, sorry! Sorry!" Mary Mary told her. "But it was your cat's fault. Your cat's —" Her words were cut off when a vine abruptly whooshed up out of her pot. However, nothing blossomed on it.

"What? What went wrong?" Mary Mary wondered aloud, staring at her blossomless plant. Rapunzel stared, too. Because it was odd that nothing had grown on it.

Ms. Blue Fairygodmother came over in her big blue bubble to help. As Rapunzel stood up and moved back to make room, a curl flopped into her face. Which was weird. Her hair hung in soft waves but was not at all curly. She brushed the curl aside. It flopped again. She brushed it back again.

"Um, Rapunzel?"

She whirled around to find Prince Perfect standing behind her. Immediately she froze, feeling her cheeks turn pink.

He shoved his hands into his pockets and shifted from one foot to the other. "You know the Festival Ball Sunday night? The one that'll be on Heart Island when the festival ends?"

"Yeah . . . uh . . . sure," she said. She and her friends had planned it. Didn't he know that? She caught sight of Mermily out of the corner of her eye, making an excited face at her. *Huh?* Why was she doing that? Then Rapunzel drew in a quick, stunned breath. *Did Mermily think he was going to ask Rapunzel to go to the ball with him? Was she right?*

Suddenly, Rapunzel felt her hair shift around. She'd used a magic spell that morning to make sure her blue braid would stay twined. Had it somehow come undone? She reached with her hands to gather her hair back up, but caught only air. Where had her hair gone? Prince Perfect was looking up at something above her head. Whatever he saw there made him stare in surprise, and then smile smugly.

"Guess I'm irresistible," he said. No, she must've misheard. He'd never say something that conceited. He sent a satisfied look in the direction of his three guys friends. Basil frowned back at him.

Soft exclamations and a few giggles reached her ears. And now Mary Mary had begun to gaze back and forth suspiciously between Rapunzel and Perfect. Mermily's eyes had gone round and wide now. Using her two forefingers, she drew an invisible heart shape in the air, then pointed to the space above Rapunzel's head.

When Rapunzel looked up, her mouth dropped open at what she saw. Her hair had somehow managed to twine itself into two long braids, which had risen high overhead to form a wiggling heart shape above her and Perfect!

She looked at him, feeling her cheeks flush. How *grimmbarrassing*! Her hair had just revealed her secret crush to the world, or at least to Perfect and all the other students in Bespellings and Enchantments. However, Ms. Blue was so intent on examining Mary Mary's plant that she didn't seem to notice Rapunzel's social life going out of control right next to her.

"I think your tongue twister sneeze gave Rapunzel's hair a case of the wiggles," Mermily said in a loud whisper to Mary Mary.

So that was it! Rapunzel reached up quickly and knocked the wiggles out of her high heart-shaped hair. The braids untwined and fell back in place to hang around her normally again.

Bong! The Hickory Dickory Dock clock began sounding the end of class. *Saved* — sort of — by the bell!

"Class dismissed," called Ms. Blue, who had seen nothing of the whole hair disaster.

As fast as she could, Rapunzel scooped up her Handbook and dashed from the room, with Mordred hard on her heels. Hoping to put the whole incident behind her, she headed for lunch in the Great Hall. There was bound to be gossip about her crushing on Perfect, though. If Mermily was right, it was all thanks to Mary Mary's wayward tongue twister spell. It had spoiled everything! Perfect would never ask her to the Festival Ball now. Because she'd just proved herself too weird, as in *not* perfect for him.

Rapunzel sighed. *Whatever.* She had more important things to worry about at the moment. Such as trying to talk Mistress Hagscorch out of making her gather that rampion!

3

Bad Hair Day

"Mistress Hagscorch?" called Rapunzel. She'd rushed straight from Bespellings to the Great Hall, arriving to find Hagscorch's fairy assistants preparing to serve lunch to the students already in line.

"She's in the kitchen," one of the fairies told her.

"Thanks," called Rapunzel. She ducked around the serving area and ran into the kitchen behind it. She looked around at the floor and walls covered with gleaming white tiles. Copper-bottomed pots and pans hung from hooks on the walls and ceilings, while others sat on the stove. Spoons, knives, corkscrews, pounders, measurers, and other utensils were scattered across countertops.

Bang! Bang! Rapunzel followed the sound to an enormous black cast-iron oven pumping out heat, against the far wall. The cook was hunched over the oven, banging out a drum solo on it with a large spoon and a wooden spatula as she peered through the glass door on its front. Whatever was baking inside the oven smelled delicious!

"Mistress Hagscorch?" Rapunzel repeated, going closer.

The cook jumped in surprise and then whipped around, blinking at her. Her face was craggy and her hands bony, but her middle was almost as round as Mr. Hump-Dumpty, the enormous egg who taught Grimm History. She wore a big starched white apron, and there was something red and gooey dripping from the spoon she held.

Was that . . . blood? Rapunzel's eyes widened and she took a step backward.

Hagscorch moved to the counter nearest the oven and waved her over with the big drippy spoon. "Come closer, dearie," she cackled. "I was just putting the finishing touches on the desserts I'll be serving in the cafeteria at dinner tonight. Heart-of-Despairberry Tarts."

"Oh, thank goodness," Rapunzel murmured under her breath. It wasn't blood after all. The red came from the berries. She moved nearer to admire the heart-shaped tarts. They were beautifully decorated with candies and icing that had been sculpted into three-dimensional scenes with fairy-tale or nursery-rhyme characters. Each was a little work of art!

"They're so lifelike. Almost too adorable to eat," Rapunzel said, admiring a scene showing a boy climbing a beanstalk sculpted from a spearmint stick. Another showed three little gumdrop kittens who'd lost their mittens, which were lying near them on the tart's snowy white frosting.

Mistress Hagscorch let out a pleased cackle and nodded in agreement. Eyes that were as yellow as a cat's sized Rapunzel up. Then the cook held out a tray of tarts. "Here. Try one. You're looking much too thin." For some strange reason, the cook was always trying to fatten up Academy students.

Rapunzel set her Handbook aside and eagerly took a tart. After all, it was lunchtime and she was pretty hungry. "Mmm. Yummy," she pronounced as she took a bite. She watched the cook work as she munched more of the snack, soon finishing it off.

When Hagscorch handed her a silver spatula, Rapunzel took the hint (and the spatula) and helped scoop the decorated tarts off the tray. They set them on fancy crystal platters that would be displayed on the dessert table at the end of the cafeteria line tonight at dinner. After a minute, Hagscorch opened the oven to reveal iron racks with more trays of tarts. She and Rapunzel lifted the trays with mitted hands onto cooling racks.

Remembering something, Rapunzel frowned. "Why are you making these tarts now? I thought they were for the festival this weekend." Despairberries had been on Hagscorch's list of things to gather earlier that week. It had taken Rapunzel *hours* to gather them from the wretched, unhappy vines that grew on the back walls of the school. The whole time she was picking the berries, the vines had restlessly wailed and writhed.

Hagscorch sniffed in a grumpy way. "Not anymore," she said, looking a little disgruntled.

"How come?"

"Because I'm serving them at dinner tonight! Weren't you listening just now? Anyway, I have another festival dessert idea in mind." She lifted an eyebrow at Rapunzel. "Which is why I asked you for some rampion. Where is it, hmm?"

Rapunzel stiffened and shook her head. "I only got your message marble in my last class. When would I have had time to pick it? Besides, you'd said you were going to make despairberry tarts for the festival."

"And now I'm going to make something else instead. Something that requires rampion." The cook's strange yellow eyes lit up like bright candles. "I've just come up with a new recipe for . . ." Her expression went shifty. "Never mind, you'll see," she finished, clamping her lips shut.

"It wasn't easy picking all those despairberries, you know," Rapunzel argued. "And it's not fair to expect me to gather a new ingredient last minute." She gestured toward the crystal platters laden with exquisitely decorated tarts. "Can't you save those tarts for this weekend? They're so cute, and you were so excited about serving them at the festival —"

"That was before I learned that a certain snooty Comportment teacher is making tarts for the festival, too!"

Hagscorch waved her spoon in irritation, flinging red berry goo over the white tile floor.

"Ms. Queenharts?"

"Exactly! If she thinks she can outshine me with her recipe and win the Best Snack Award at that festival, she's got another think coming. *I'm* the queen of cooks at this Academy!"

Rapunzel trailed after her across the kitchen, where she set the tray she'd just emptied onto a metal counter. There were more trays of tarts there waiting to be baked, so she and the cook picked them up, went back to the oven, and slid the tarts inside. Before closing the oven door, Hagscorch gazed tenderly at the new tarts as if they were her babies and she was putting them to bed. "Cook well, little tarts!" she cooed.

Mistress Hagscorch prided herself on her cooking, so Rapunzel could understand why it would irritate and embarrass her if Ms. Queenharts's tarts outdid hers at the festival. People from all over Grimmlandia were coming. Hagscorch wouldn't want to risk humiliation.

"The thing is, I can't do what you've requested," Rapunzel went on. Desperate, she fibbed, "I don't know where to find rampion."

"Don't be ridiculous. You can find any plant, no matter how rare, and we both know it. You once found a patch of five-leaf clovers for me!" The cook eyed her. "You're not trying to pop-goes-the-*weasel* out of that bargain we made at the beginning of the year, are you? The one where I don't tell anyone that your task is Gatherer, and in return for my silence, you gather whatever I need whenever I need it?"

"Well . . ." Rapunzel began. Students were required to perform their school-assigned tasks only once a week, and the cook had never taken advantage and asked her to do more. Until now.

Just then, two lunch fairies flitted in. Together, they picked up and then carried off a crystal platter of despair-berry tarts, probably to set in the front case. There the platter would sit and tantalize students with what was to come for dinner that night. The tarts moaned wretchedly — which was typical despairberry behavior — as they were taken away.

Rapunzel felt like moaning, too. She'd made two bad bargains in her life, and her deal with Hagscorch was one of them. Too late, she tried to argue her way out of it. "I'm busy, you know. I have school, plus there's the festival to help plan. Besides, the only place rampion grows is in Neverwood, which is . . ." *Oops.* Now she'd revealed that she *did* know where to find rampion!

Hagscorch only shrugged. "You'll figure something out. Be sure to take one of your little Grimm girl friends with you. Neverwood Forest isn't a place you should be wandering about on your own, especially in the dark."

36

Rapunzel's jaw dropped. Hagscorch wanted her to go to that eerie forest to search for herbs *tonight*? She must be despairing as much as those despairberries about the upcoming cooking contest. Otherwise she'd never suggest such a thing.

"Why don't you make Rattlebone Scones instead?" Rapunzel coaxed in a last-ditch effort to change the cook's mind. "Everyone loves those. Or your Huffing Puffs or your Doomdogs and Gloomburgers."

"Yes, yes. I'll bake a variety of snacks, but I want to offer something new as well. Something spectacular. A crowd-pleaser." Her eyes took on a faraway look as she went on. "A glorious centerpiece item that will blow Ms. Fancy-pants Queenharts's tarts out of the water. Which is why I thought of a ship."

"Ship?" Rapunzel echoed.

Hagscorch covered her lips with an oven-mitted hand. "Oh, cramshackle! I didn't mean to tell. But now that you know, I'll have to trust you to keep mum. I'm calling it the Rampion Championship," she confided happily. "It's a one-of-a-kind dessert that will be awarded to whoever Principal R chooses as the champion of all champions at the festival games!"

Principal Rumpelstiltskin, she meant. But nobody ever called him that. It was strictly against Rule 37 in the GA Handbook to do so. Even *he* couldn't say his own name without sparking himself into a fit. Which was why, on Cinda's very first day at GA, she had nicknamed him Grumpystiltskin!

Rapunzel wrinkled her nose. "But who wants to eat ship-shaped spinach for dessert? Or get it for a prize?"

Hagscorch arched an eyebrow. "Maybe you should crack open that Handbook of yours and study up on rampion."

Curious, Rapunzel grabbed her Handbook from the table where she'd laid it and did as the cook suggested. "Encyclopedia . . . look up *rampion*," she commanded, pushing the GA oval on its cover.

Her Handbook opened and swiftly fanned to the word she sought. She skimmed down its description. Then her finger stopped. " 'When eaten, rampion offers a taste of what a person most desires,' " she read aloud. She shut her book and looked at the cook quizzically. "Whatever they most desire?"

Hagscorch let out a huge cackle. "Rampion may belong to the spinach family, but it doesn't taste like spinach, or even like food necessarily. The taste might give one person a glimpse of home or of a loved one. Or lead them to find a desired object such as a jewel beyond compare. With magic like that, my Rampion Championship is sure to be more popular than any old tarts a certain Comportment teacher can bake!"

Rapunzel stood there, feeling stunned. In her fairy tale, her mom had asked her dad to steal some rampion, even knowing it belonged to a witch — and knowing there would be consequences. So what had her mother's heart most desired all those years ago? What had she wanted so badly that she was willing to give Rapunzel away to a witch in order to get it?

Yellow eyes narrowed at her. "Don't let me down. You know what happens to students who don't fulfill their tower tasks."

"Demerits," Rapunzel replied. According to Rule 83 in the GA Handbook, too many of them meant expulsion from the Academy.

The cook pointed her spoon at Rapunzel. "Exactly! Now run along," she ordered. "You're my best Gatherer and I'm depending on you — so quit trying to wiggle out of your duty and go gather what I need. By tonight!" Leaving the tarts baking, Hagscorch headed off for the lunch line — to terrorize some other poor kids, no doubt.

Oomph! Rapunzel staggered backward as if someone had pushed her. But no one had. Her hair had gone wiggly again, jerking her this way and that. Oh, no! Hagscorch had accidentally said the bad-magic word: *wiggle*!

"Wait," said Rapunzel, following her despite her hair problems. She was not going back to that despised rampion patch. Nuh-uh. She had to figure some way out of this task — fast.

"Can't one of the other Gatherers get it for you?" she protested.

"They're all busy with other tasks," Hagscorch called back over her shoulder. "I want you to do it. Besides, you have a knack for finding things that my other Gatherers don't."

In a flash, another idea came to Rapunzel. "What if I can talk Ms. Queenharts out of making tarts for the festival?" she blurted.

Hagscorch stopped at the entrance to the serving area and turned to stare at her doubtfully. Then suddenly, a look of total surprise filled her face. "What's wrong with your hair?" she demanded.

Rapunzel glanced up in time to see her hair reach out, curl around the handles of two pans, and begin banging them together. *Clang! Crash!* "Sorry! Tongue twister spell malfunction in Bespellings class," she explained quickly as she pulled the pans from her hair's clutches. "So about Ms. Queenharts . . ."

Wap! Clang! More locks of her hair had wiggled out, nabbed some pots from their hooks, and started juggling them!

"I can't have your hair acting up like this in here," yelled Hagscorch. She reached out and grabbed hold of another hunk of Rapunzel's hair as it headed for the crystal platters of tarts. "No, you don't," she scolded, reeling it in. "I don't want *hair*berry tarts! That's not sanitary!"

She's one to talk, thought Rapunzel as she tried to get control of her tresses. Hagscorch's white-gray hair was as wild and scraggly as the moss that grew at the edge of Neverwood.

"Out!" yelled the cook, pointing toward the kitchen door.

"Okay! Yeah! Sorry," said Rapunzel. After prying loose the last of the pots and pans, she scuttled out of the kitchen and ran past the lunch line. She burst out into the Great Hall, a long room that was two stories high and straddled the Once Upon River. The Hall was full of students now. Some were in the lunch line; others were still straggling in from classes. Several dozen already had trays of food and were seated at the two tables that stretched the entire length of the room.

Fleeing, Rapunzel made a beeline for the entrance to Pink Castle at the far end of the Hall. Unfortunately, she could tell her hair still had a case of the wiggles. What was it doing up there? Heads turned, staring. She shot a *Yikes, I don't know what's happening* look to her three BFFs, who were just sitting down to eat at their usual table as she ran past. A lock of her hair whipped toward them, and then sprang back just as quickly.

Whack! Meanwhile, another lock of her hair had reached out and knocked a chair onto the floor. "Hey, watch it!" exclaimed Princess Pea, who'd been about to sit there.

"Is it snowing?" Rapunzel heard someone ask. She glanced over to see that her hair had picked up a saltshaker from a table and was sprinkling salt over some of the students. Next, it picked up some bread sticks and tossed them into the air. Briefly, they curved and aligned to shape two-foot-tall letters — *R + P* — above her head before dropping back to the table.

Students began whispering, probably wondering who the *P* stood for. They'd find out soon enough when someone from her Bespellings class told them about the heart-shaped hair incident. She passed a group of guys at one table. Basil was among them, and he was staring at her with a concerned look. Some of the people around him, including Cinda's two mean stepsisters, were giggling. This was sooo *grimmorrible*!

Eventually, Rapunzel reached the hall exit that led to Pink Castle. She heard the sound of breaking glass behind her, but ran on, not even stopping to see what had happened. Whatever it was, it was likely her hair's fault!

And her troubles were far from over. Out in the first-floor hall of Pink Castle, her hair knocked books from hands. *Wham! Wham!* It shut trunkers just opened. *Slam! Slam!*

At last, she pulled open a door to the grand staircase, then another just inside the landing. Down the stairs she flew, then through a tunnel that finally ended at her dungeon door. She unlocked it and zipped inside, dashing across the stone floor to look into the tall oval mirror that hung on her armoire. She stared at her reflection in dismay. Her hair had truly gone wild! It wiggled. It waved. It stood out from her head like a half dozen long, fat, squirmy worms.

She flung open the armoire's double doors. A variety of brushes, combs, ribbons, clips, and scissors were stacked, stowed, or hung neatly inside, all sorted by color and style. After grabbing a random brush, she slammed the doors shut again. Gazing into the mirror, she frantically began to run the brush through her hair in an attempt to tame her unruly mane.

Her five cats had been sleeping, but now they perked up. Intrigued by anything that wiggled, Mordred jumped from the sill of the high window where he'd been dozing, down to the top of the armoire. Then he peered at her, batting at her writhing hair.

At the same time, her white cat, Moon, jumped onto her trunk. From there the cat leaped to join Mordred atop the armoire.

Her fluffy gray cat, Shadow, and her two solid black cats, Raven and Midnight, prowled around on the floor, gazing up at her with interest. Whenever a lock of her glossy dark hair ventured low enough to reach, they took a swat at it with their furry paws.

Still brandishing her brush, Rapunzel sent them all a wry, affectionate smile. "I'm glad *someone's* enjoying my predicament."

Knock. Knock. Knock.

Now what? she wondered, going to the door. Hardly anyone ever bothered her down here. Most people thought the dungeon was kind of creepy. But she liked it, despite its drawbacks. For instance, sometimes she got left out of dorm activities since she usually wasn't up in the tower when they took place. Still, she wouldn't want to live any-where else. Given her phobia of heights, the trade-off was worth it — most of the time.

She opened the little hinged window in her room's door and peeked through its bars.

"It's me," Snow called. "I mean *us*. Cinda, Red, and me." When Rapunzel opened the door, her friends gaped at her hair in astonishment.

"What —?" asked Red. Her dark brown eyes were filled with worry.

"It started in Bespellings and Enchantments," Rapunzel explained, zooming back to the mirror so she could con-tinue brushing her hair. "Mary Mary sneezed a tongue twister at me with a certain word spelled w-i-g-g-l-e. And now any time someone says that word, voilà! My hair goes bonkers."

"Mermily told us," said Cinda, nodding. "And we saw the results ourselves just now in the Hall. Any ideas on how to fix this hairy problem?" The girls shut the door behind them and came over to join Rapunzel at the mirror.

"You could shave it off and wear a hat for a while," Snow suggested in a half-joking way. She stepped to one side of the mirror so she couldn't see her own reflection. Mirrors weirded her out.

Rapunzel's wiggly hair momentarily froze as if horrified by the very idea of being shaved off. The idea horrified Rapunzel as well. Though she wouldn't be bald for long, given how fast her hair grew.

"I think I'll just brush out the tangles," she replied. Her hair started wiggling again as if it was relieved to hear that. "But if I get really desperate, you never know!"

"What can we do to help? Do you have any more brushes or combs?" asked Cinda.

"In there," said Rapunzel, gesturing toward the left side of her armoire. Since Snow was closest, she opened its door.

Cinda, who'd been in this room only twice since coming to the Academy at the start of the year, gasped when she saw all the ribbons, brushes, and other hair care items stored inside. "Wow!"

"Rapunzel collects hair stuff like I collect lucky stuff," said Snow, who wore a four-leaf clover amulet on the key chain around her neck. She reached for a comb and so did Cinda. Red selected a brush.

The three girls gathered around Rapunzel and began helping her comb and brush out the wiggly tangles.

"It's like taming a hairy octopus!" Red said at one point.

"Yeah. An octopus that's also a thief," said Cinda.

She was right. As they wrestled Rapunzel's hair, they pulled out small things that it had picked up in the Great Hall. A saltshaker, several spoons, someone's teacup, a napkin, and a tiara.

"Hey! That's my magic charm!" said Snow, pulling the tiara free. "Your hair must've lassoed it. It was on the table when you passed, but I didn't even notice it happening!"

"Sorry," said Rapunzel.

"Maybe you'd better check your basket for the *You Know What*," Cinda advised Red.

"You can call it a mapestry in here," Rapunzel told her as she untangled a quill pen from her hair. "No one's around but us and the cats."

"Oh, right," said Cinda. "It's just that I'm so used to having to keep it secret."

Rapunzel watched Red's reflection in the mirror as the girl went over to her basket on the bed, where she'd set it when she came in.

"It's here," Red assured them after opening her basket, which snuggled up to her side like a happy puppy as she withdrew the magical stitched tapestry map.

"I think it's calming down," Snow noted in a whisper.

"Um-hmm," Cinda agreed.

Rapunzel's gaze shifted to her reflection in the mirror and saw that they were talking about her hair, which indeed finally hung around her normally now. She, Snow, and Cinda each took a third of it. Threading ribbons through it in a decorative way that also kept it securely bound, they wove the three sections into a single braid that hung down to the back of her knees.

"It looks cute," Cinda pronounced at last.

"And peaceful," said Snow. "I do believe we tamed it!"

Rapunzel shook her head from side to side. When her hair didn't break free from the ribbons, she nodded, pleased and relieved. Snow opened her mouth to say more but was interrupted by Red.

"The X hasn't moved from Heart Island," Red noted. She had unrolled the mapestry atop the comforter covering the bed and was studying it. "It must mean the treasure is still there, waiting." Working on the island to set up the festival had given them plenty of chances to look for treasure, but so far they hadn't found it.

Rapunzel, Snow, and Cinda joined Red over by the bed to gaze at the mapestry. Raven and Midnight hopped on the bed, too, and curled up together on the comforter. Meanwhile, Moon and Shadow had fallen asleep on the armoire. Mordred threaded between the girls' legs, then crawled under the bed, where he sometimes liked to nap.

Red put her fingertip on the *X* that was cross-stitched in golden thread atop a heart-shaped island north of the Academy. At the same time, the clock over in the Great Hall began to bong. The sound echoed throughout the school, signaling the end of lunch.

"Fourth period? Already?" Rapunzel said nervously. She was a little worried about her hair acting up in her afternoon classes.

"Oh! We forgot to tell you," said Cinda. "A few minutes after you left the Hall, Principal R came out on the balcony and made an announcement that afternoon classes are canceled today and tomorrow."

"So that everyone at GA can get ready for the festival," added Red. "A bunch of people are going to head over to Heart Island right away."

"Yeah, including teachers. I'm supposed to meet my stepmom there soon," said Snow. Her stepmom, Ms. Wicked, taught Scrying at the Academy, which was the art of seeing the future with the use of reflective objects. The girls had recently discovered that she also secretly belonged to the E.V.I.L. Society!

Determination rose in Rapunzel when she heard about the canceled classes and the teachers going to the island. This might be her only chance to try to talk Ms. Queenharts out of making those tarts before the festival began on Saturday. Mistress Hagscorch hadn't exactly said no to the idea, after all.

"I've been waiting all day for us to be alone so I could tell you guys something alarming," Snow added in a hushed voice. "I sneaked a peek at my stepmom's calendar. And guess what she wrote in the date box for this coming Monday. Three words: *GA is ours.*"

"Huh? What does that mean?" wondered Red. Then she paled, coming up with the answer herself. "That must be the day E.V.I.L. plans to take over the Academy!"

"Not if we can help it," Cinda rushed to say. "If the festival earns enough money to pay the school's debts this weekend, they can't take it from us, right?"

"We can only hope," said Rapunzel.

"Well, what are we waiting for? There's festival stuff to do." Red rolled up the mapestry and tucked it back in her basket.

"Yeah, let's go," said Rapunzel. Instead of going through the door with the barred window and leading the girls up the tunnel, she went to the curved stone wall on the opposite side of her room. She'd painted it with a mural of a nighttime forest scene in various shades of black, silver, and white. Bats and owls flitted through a moonlit sky while heavy-limbed trees swayed below them. There was a small, real window tucked among the painted trees that gave her a view of Heart Island in the distance.

And cleverly disguised in some painted shrubbery on one side of the mural, about waist-high, there was a doorknob. Rapunzel reached out and turned it.

4

Heart Island

When the knob in the mural opened a door to the outside, Cinda gasped. "How clever! You disguised it so well that I didn't even know there was another door to your room."

Rapunzel smiled and led her three BFFs out into the sunlight and up some old crumbly stone steps. When they reached ground level, they were only a short distance from the river, where a swan-shaped boat was docked. The boat's bright white paint was a striking contrast to the deep, rich blue waters of the Once Upon River. There were other swan boats docked along the river, but most were across from the drawbridges at either end of the Academy.

"Think we'll find the treasure this afternoon?" asked Snow as they stepped into the boat.

"Might be hard to do much looking with so many people around," Rapunzel noted. She sat next to Snow on one of the boat's two bench seats, facing Cinda and Red.

Cinda nodded. "Yeah, it would be easier if that stitched

X on the mapestry were more exact. Basically, the treasure could be anywhere on Heart Island."

"I just hope one of *them* doesn't discover it first!" said Red. The others had each picked up an oar and now she took the remaining one. "Them" was the girls' code-speak for the E.V.I.L. Society. The mysterious and villainous Society had existed around the time the Grimm brothers founded Grimmlandia, but it had later died out. For some unknown reason, it had recently begun to operate again. And now it seemed bent on weakening the magical wall around Grimmlandia that had kept all the fairy-tale and nursery-rhyme characters safe within its borders for more than a century!

"That won't happen as long as we've got the true mapestry," Snow reminded them. Her stepmom had an identical but false one that Snow had embroidered herself, with a little help from some magical dwarves. But that fake mapestry would only lead Ms. Wicked on a wild goose chase.

"At least no more artifacts have gone over the wall lately," said Rapunzel. She dipped her oar into the river, and the girls began paddling for Heart Island.

"Yeah, nothing since Peter Peter Pumpkineater's coach and Jack and Jill's pail," said Cinda. "Just think — if that pumpkin hadn't taken the seeds of prosperity with it, we wouldn't have needed to plan a festival. Not that it hasn't been fun, of course. And I think everyone will have a great time on Saturday."

The stolen pumpkin was the reason the Academy was in financial trouble. Unfortunately, the GA Handbook clearly stated that they couldn't sell any of the Academy's vast riches to bail the school out of its financial difficulties, so the girls had come up with the festival as a way to earn much-needed funds instead.

Artifacts from the Grimmstone Library had begun to disappear recently, which had led to the weakening of Grimmlandia's protective wall. No one knew how many artifacts it might take to weaken the wall enough that the E.V.I.L. Society's leader — as well as beasts and dastardlies that lurked outside the wall — could break through it and take control of Grimmlandia. Or even if that was really the society's plan. But the Grimm girls and Principal R were all very worried and were trying to make sure no more arti-facts got stolen.

"Speaking of *them*," said Snow. "When we reach Heart Island, I'm supposed to go treasure-hunting with my step-mom, using the fake mapestry. Luckily, I think she's buying my act that I'm willing to help her find the treasure. And by the way, we were right. She *isn't* planning to give any trea-sure she might find to E.V.I.L."

"I knew it! She wants to keep it for herself," said Red.

"Her double-crossing makes her even more evil than the Society itself, if you ask me," added Rapunzel.

Suddenly, Snow let out a bloodcurdling cackle. A jolt of alarm swept the others, and the boat rocked in the water.

"Why'd you do that?" asked Cinda.

"Just practicing my evil laugh," Snow explained. "In case I need it to fool my stepmom."

"Well, you're a little *too* good at it!" Red said with a shiver.

Snow glanced at her, a hint of worry in her green eyes.

"Only kidding," Red assured her. They all knew she had once suspected Snow of being on the side of E.V.I.L., but the girls truly trusted one another now.

"So let's talk festival business," said Cinda. "Everyone got their lists? I'll go first," she said as lists were pulled from pockets, a sparkly blue bag, and a basket. "The locations for the sports competitions are all set and scheduled. Coach Candlestick will be hosting the candlestick-jumping competition," she noted, looking down her list. "And we've got hip-hop-scotch. And there's the masketball game on Saturday afternoon." Cinda and her crush, Prince Awesome, were star players at masketball, a game where players wore masks and shot balls at hoops on magical goals that moved around the court on their own.

"The pet show is pretty much organized," Rapunzel reported. "Lots of kids around Grimmlandia are entering, and they'll all get prizes. I've made ribbons for things like brownest pet, pet with the longest ears, the longest whiskers, the greenest eyes. Stuff like that. Oh, and Basil said he and his friends are working on some kind of ride or game or something," she told Snow, who was in charge of the rides and games. "But he wouldn't tell me what it is. He wants to surprise us."

"Cool, I'll add it to the list," said Snow. "The rest of the rides and games are taken care of. We've got bumper coaches, dart games, catapults, swan boat races. Plus Ms. Blue Fairygodmother is making big magical colored bubble balls so people can roll down Jack and Jill Hill inside them."

"How fun! I'd pay to do that," said Cinda.

"Me, too," Red and Snow added at the same time. "Jinx," they both said, quickly hooking pinkies.

Next, Red read aloud from her check-marked to-do list. "Scenic backdrops set up on the island's amphitheater stage: check," she said. She and Wolfgang were such good actors that both had scored the lead roles in *Red Robin Hood*, the school play. They planned to perform it at the festival so that all of Grimmlandia could enjoy it. "Play ready to open Saturday night on amphitheater stage around sunset: check. And Ms. Jabberwocky, Ms. Queenharts, and Mistress Hagscorch making plenty of snacks during the play and throughout the festival: check."

At the mention of the cook's name, Rapunzel made a face.

"What's wrong?" Cinda asked.

"Nothing," Rapunzel replied quickly. She wished she could tell her BFFs about her rampion problem. She didn't like keeping secrets from them. And maybe they could help. But would they think differently about her if they knew the truth? That her job was being a Gatherer — a *witch's* task?

And there was an even worse secret she held. Something truly terrible that loomed in her future. But she definitely didn't want to tell them or anyone about *that*. In fact, she'd tried not to even think about it herself during all the years she'd been at GA.

"I think we've covered pretty much everything," said Red, as they all tucked their lists away again. "The rides, the food, the games, the pets, the drama. Now here's hoping the festival is a big success so we can pay off the school's debts!"

"Yay!" they all cheered. That's what the festival was really for, of course. But they also hoped it would be fun.

As their swan boat pulled up to Heart Island and they hopped out onto the dock, people began coming up to them with questions about festival business. The Grimm girls were drawn off in different directions to check out the various activities they were responsible for.

Almost immediately, Rapunzel spotted a teacher wearing a dress covered with white, pink, and red hearts, and wearing a small red crown. Ms. Queenharts. She was in one of the three big, white, wrought-iron gazebos that would be used as food booths for the festival. "I'll go see how the food preparations are coming," Rapunzel volunteered to Red. "That'll free you to make sure all is on schedule for the *Red Robin Hood* performance at the amphitheater."

Red nodded gratefully. Putting on a festival was a lot of work and they all had to help each other.

"Hi, Ms. Queenharts," Rapunzel called out a minute later as she approached the gazebo where the teacher was setting up her food booth. Ms. Jabberwocky and Mistress Hagscorch would set up in the other two gazebos nearby. Neither of them was here yet, though. Now was Rapunzel's chance.

Ms. Queenharts only huffed in response to her greeting as she reached into one of the trunks she'd brought to the island. Then she turned and looked down her long nose at Rapunzel.

"Help me set the tables," the teacher demanded, handing her a stack of starched, frilly white napkins that she'd pulled from the trunk. Together, they began setting them at places all around the linen-draped tables.

"Isn't it a little early to set places?" Rapunzel asked as they worked. "The festival doesn't begin till the day after tomorrow."

Ms. Queenharts sniffed haughtily. "I don't know how things are done where you come from, young lady. However, it is proper etiquette in Wonderland to be prepared for guests who may arrive early," she replied in a superior tone. She was fond of reminding everyone that she had come to GA from Wonderland, a very hoity-toity neighborhood in the realm of Grimmlandia.

Each place mat on the table was embroidered in fancy gold thread, Rapunzel noticed as she set out the napkins. Stitched upon them were the words: *Good comportment means behaving in a polite and princely or princessly manner whether or not one is a prince or princess.*

Ha! Although Ms. Queenharts taught Comportment — which was basically the same as manners — she certainly wasn't polite herself!

As Rapunzel worked, the teacher went to another trunk and pulled out a crystal tray — a special kind used to display tarts. *Oh, no!*

"You know those cupcakes you made in class during silverware placement studies?" Rapunzel said quickly. Ms. Queenharts ignored her and just kept working.

Rapunzel rushed on. "Well, I don't know if you heard, but everyone simply *loved* those cupcakes of yours, including me. And since my friends and I are in charge of the festival, including the food booths, I was just wondering if I could ask you to make them as desserts this weekend?"

Ms. Queenharts whipped around to stare at her. "Did Mistress Hagscorch put you up to this?" she demanded.

"Huh? Who? No!" Rapunzel tried to sound innocent, but she felt her cheeks warm. She'd told the truth, though, because asking Ms. Queenharts to make something else had been *her* idea, not Hagscorch's.

"It's just that your cupcakes were so tasty," she rushed on. "And Mistress Hagscorch is also planning tarts, so I thought . . ."

"Aha!" Ms. Queenharts exclaimed, pointing a silver spoon at her. "I was right! Don't try to wiggle out of this one. The two of you must be in cahoots, and . . ."

She rambled on, but Rapunzel was too distracted to listen. Because the minute the word *wiggle* hung in the air between them, she'd felt a slight jiggle at her back. Her hair. *Not now! Not again!*

Panicking, she quickly plopped down on the bench at the nearest table, sitting atop her single braid. It wriggled around some. But then, seeming to realize she had it pinned, it gave up on making trouble. For now, at least. How long was she going to have to worry about it going wackadoodle every time someone spoke the word *wiggle*? she wondered. Mary Mary's accidental spell would wear off eventually, wouldn't it? Reluctantly, she tuned back in to what Ms. Queenharts was saying.

"Do you know why I'm making tarts for the festival?

Because *I*" — Ms. Queenharts paused dramatically and pointed the spoon at herself — "am the *Queen* of Tarts! You must have heard my nursery rhyme. The one where I made some tarts all on a summer's day? And what else happened that day? Mistress Hagscorch, that's what. She sent a knave to steal those tarts and take them clean away!"

So! This old misunderstanding was at the heart of the trouble between Ms. Queenharts and Hagscorch, thought Rapunzel. "Are you sure it was her — that *she* sent the knave?" she asked. "Maybe it was his own idea. Maybe he was hungry. I mean, why would she want your tarts when she can make her own?"

"For the recipe, you dolt! It's a secret that has been handed down for generations in my family. However," — Ms. Queenharts paused briefly to lift more napkins from her trunk. Then she went on — "if you can get her to admit she stole the recipe and hired a knave to steal my tarts, I won't make them for the festival after all. Deal?"

"Uh, I guess so," said Rapunzel. She sighed inwardly, setting both elbows on the tabletop and resting her chin on her hands. She'd have to become the queen of fancy bargaining to make Hagscorch do any such thing. There was no way.

"Off with your elbows!" yelled Ms. Queenharts. "I mean — elbows off the table!" Startled, Rapunzel drew back, setting her hands in her lap. The teacher smoothed imaginary rumples from the tablecloth, saying, "We must avoid wrinkles and tears in our linens, as well as our gowns and tunics!"

"Will you at least think about the cupcakes?" Rapunzel asked, standing and stepping away from the table. She was getting a headache from the teacher's yelling. Didn't she know how to speak in normal tones?

Ms. Queenharts aimed her narrowed eyes in the direction of Rapunzel's hair. "It's a good thing tomorrow's lesson in class is on good grooming."

Huh? Oh, fragwaggle! thought Rapunzel. The minute she'd stood, her hair had begun wiggling again at her back, trying to unbraid itself. She grabbed the now-straggly braid and wrapped it around her waist, holding it tight with both hands. She didn't dare remind Ms. Queenharts that she took Comportment in the afternoon, and afternoon classes had been canceled due to festival preparations. The very last thing she wanted to do was to fan the teacher's temper, which was almost as bad as Principal Rumpelstiltskin's!

"Every hair must be kept in place," shouted Ms. Queenharts. "Either get yourself under control or . . . off with your hair! Off with your hair!" With an imperious gesture, she grabbed a rose from one of the table centerpieces with her left hand and nabbed a silver butter knife with her right. *Whack!* She sliced off the flower's head, leaving only its long stem.

Rapunzel's eyes widened in shock. Fortunately, her hair seemed shocked, too. It stopped its wiggling and hung calmly at her back again.

"Hey!" called a voice. Cinda had come over to rescue her. *Thank grimmness!* She smiled at Ms. Queenharts as she grabbed Rapunzel's hand and started tugging her away. "C'mon. You need to see what Basil and Awesome and their friends have done."

"Okay," said Rapunzel. She sent Ms. Queenharts one last beseeching glance. "Think about making those cupcakes of yours, okay?" Not waiting to hear the teacher's reply, she allowed Cinda to pull her from the gazebo.

Together the two Grimm girls crossed the smooth green lawn, where siege engines were being set up for a planned demonstration. They kept moving toward the opposite end of the island from the food gazebos. When they rounded a grove of tall trees, Rapunzel looked up ahead . . . and stopped dead. Stunned by what she saw in the distance, she just stood there staring, her hand sliding from Cinda's grasp.

There was a new addition to the festival entertainment. And in her opinion, it was a very unwelcome one!

5

The Witch

Rapunzel stared in horror at the tall stone tower standing among the trees.

"What's wrong?" Cinda asked, backtracking to her side.

"Nothing," Rapunzel lied quickly. But her heart was thumping louder than the *bongs* the grandfather clock in the Great Hall could make. She could hardly believe she hadn't noticed this tower earlier. She'd been so busy concentrating on Ms. Queenharts and the tarts that she hadn't glanced in this direction.

"C'mon," she said, and the two girls raced the rest of the way to the tower. She wanted to inspect it up close. Could it really be the witch's — *her* witch's — tower as she suspected?

Lots of students were milling around, most discussing the tower in admiring tones. It soared forty feet tall and was topped with a pointy roof that resembled a witch's hat. There were five coils of long, sturdy rope lying on the ground alongside it.

How? When? Who? So many questions clogged Rapunzel's throat.

"It appeared on this spot just this morning," someone said, gazing up at the tower.

"Where's its door?" someone else asked. "Looks like the only way in or out is that little window way up top."

Rapunzel could've told them that there was a single hidden door that would appear and open if you spoke special magic words. And that once inside the tower, you'd be trapped! Because that door wouldn't reopen to let you out again no matter what magic words you tried or how you begged.

While Cinda talked to some other kids, Rapunzel circled the base of the tower. On the far side, she found Basil and four princes at work: Perfect, Foulsmell, Awesome, and Prince.

Still kind of embarrassed over that whole hair-heart thing in Bespellings class, she avoided Perfect's eyes. Instead she went over to Foulsmell, who was seated on a tree stump. There was a bottle of ink beside him and a big sheet of vellum in his lap. With careful strokes from a quill pen, he appeared to be making a sign for an easel that Basil was setting up in front of the tower. Hand-lettered in calligraphy, the sign read: *Tower of Doom.*

That's for sure! thought Rapunzel. Little did they know that this tower represented her own doomed future. Now that she was this close to it, she was absolutely certain it was the witch's tower. Where she'd lived as a little girl, raised by that very same witch.

"How did it get here?" she asked Basil, gesturing toward the stone tower.

"Strange story," he said as he and the other boys began uncoiling the ropes at the foot of the tower and tying a stone to the end of each. "The guys and I met this really old lady in Neverwood Forest when we were looking for wood to build some kind of exhibit for this weekend. When we told her about the festival and how it was a fund-raiser for Grimm Academy, she got really interested. She told us we could use this tower till Sunday night. True to her word, she magicked it over here this very morning."

"That lady — was she a witch?"

"Probably," he said, grinning.

"Calling it the Tower of Doom was our idea," Prince Prince told her. "Cool, huh?"

Rapunzel nodded, her mind racing. "Yeah, uh-huh, cool." The witch couldn't have moved the tower here by herself. Her magic wasn't strong enough. So who had helped her? It must've been someone very powerful. Someone as evil as she, probably. Rapunzel crossed her arms, shivering.

"Are you cold? Want my cloak?" Basil asked.

She shook her head. "Did she ask for something in exchange? Make some sort of deal with you?"

He sent her his patented *Are you crazy?* look. "No way. I know better than to make a bargain with a witch."

Lucky for you, thought Rapunzel. She'd been only six years old when, like her parents, she'd made a terrible bargain with the witch. A promise she would soon have to honor but did *not* want to keep. Yet she must, unless she could wiggle out of it somehow. She hunched her shoulders, hoping her hair hadn't heard her think the word *wiggle*. But it stayed in place. *Phew!*

Thunk! Thunk! She watched Basil and his friends take turns tossing the stone ends of their ropes upward, trying to land them inside the high window. The idea seemed to be that the stones would act as anchors once over the windowsill, catching on the ledge when the boys pulled down on the free ends of the ropes. Then anyone could climb up a rope to enter through the tower window. The boys' tosses had gotten nowhere near the window so far, though. Their ropes always fell to the ground again.

"Once we secure these ropes in that window up there, we're going to let people scale the tower and try to make it inside," Basil told her.

"Yeah, tickets for a chance to climb it are selling like hotcakes. Or maybe more like Hagscorch's knick-knack paddy-whack pancakes!" Foulsmell enthused.

"Great idea, don't you think?" added Awesome.

"No!" said Rapunzel.

Everyone nearby stared at her.

"Why?" asked Red. She and Wolfgang had come over from the amphitheater to check out the tower everyone was talking about.

"Yeah, it sounds like a winner to me," Wolfgang agreed.

"I just meant that, even though she let us borrow it for the festival, it doesn't mean she'll want people tramping all over inside it. You know how cranky witches can be when you cross them," Rapunzel said. She had to convince everyone to stay away from this tower!

"Phooey," Foulsmell told her. He'd finished the sign and now set it on its easel. "Even witches know that towers are for climbing."

"And I'm betting I'll be the first to make it up this one!" Basil challenged the others.

"You're on!" said Wolfgang.

"I don't *think* so," sniffed Perfect. "Because *I* have had climbing lessons." Rapunzel saw Awesome roll his eyes, but she was sure Perfect hadn't meant to sound boastful.

Thunk! Thunk! The boys continued pitching their ropes. Each time, they flew higher.

Rapunzel groaned. She stared at Foulsmell's sign, focusing on the word *doom, Doom, DOOM*! Sometimes boys could be so clueless.

The witch had a reason for everything she did. Rapunzel was sure that her reason for letting them borrow the tower was *not* because she wanted to help with the festival. Not a chance. So why had she sent it here to Heart Island? Did she want students to go inside it? What if they all got trapped for six years like she had? Worry for her Grimm girl friends and the whole Academy filled her. Including Basil, too. After all, she'd saved him from that bully years ago and still felt kind of responsible for him.

Hearing hammering, she glanced over to see Mr. Hump-Dumpty, the giant egg who taught Grimm History, posting a sign under the tower that read:

DANGER!
BE CAREFUL ON THE TOWER
For if you fall to the ground while climbing it,
all the king's horses and all the king's men
won't be able to put you together again!

He was so right. This tower was dangerous! Slowly, Rapunzel began backing away from the group around it. She didn't want to go anywhere near that witch or her rampion patch, but she had to find out what the crabby old crone was plotting. When it seemed no one was looking her way, Rapunzel turned and headed for the swan boats.

After hopping into a small two-seater, she paddled across the river. Away from Heart Island. Away from the Academy. Toward the deep, dark Neverwood Forest. At the edge of that very scary forest, she docked her boat. Fueled with determination, she clambered out of it and started into the woods.

Rapunzel slowed as she eventually drew near her goal, a clearing up ahead. The rampion there still grew thick on the ground where it had always been, its green stalks dotted with pale purple bellflowers. In the center of the rampion patch, there was only a round flattened area to show where the tower usually stood. It was over on the island for the festival now, of course.

None of her BFFs knew she'd once lived here in that exact tower. They probably thought the tower mentioned in her tale was in some faraway corner of Grimmlandia. If only! She had purposely avoided this part of the forest ever since she'd left it to enroll at Grimm Academy.

The minute Rapunzel stepped among the rampion stalks, a cackly voice rang out. "Who's that trespassing on my property?"

Suddenly, not four feet away, the witch appeared in a puff of smoke! She looked just as Rapunzel remembered her. Long white hair, black robes, and a black brimmed hat with a tall corkscrew point.

"Rapunzel!" the witch exclaimed with delight. She smiled, showing a row of pointy, pea-green teeth. "I was hoping you'd come. And I'm so pleased to see that your hair still grows long." The witch knew very well why that was.

She'd put a spell on it years ago while Rapunzel dwelled in the tower, causing her hair to grow to great lengths so the witch could use it as a ladder to climb up and down from the tower's small window. The tower door was only for emergencies, for the witch feared that someone might see her use it and try to rescue her captive.

Rapunzel crossed her arms. Though the witch was acting friendly enough, Rapunzel knew from the evil glint in her eye that she was up to something. But what?

"Why did you lend your tower to the boys at the Academy for the festival?" Rapunzel demanded. "What did you trick them into promising you in return?"

"Nothing," the witch said. She spread her arms wide, trying to look well-meaning and innocent. Things she definitely wasn't! "I only sent the tower because I knew you'd come visit me to ask that very question. We haven't talked since you were six. I wanted to be sure you still remember our bargain."

Rapunzel just stared at her. Fortunately, her hair wasn't wiggling at the moment. How the witch would laugh at her if it did. She was unkind that way.

The black-hatted crone stepped closer. "You *do* remember our bargain, don't you?" she asked, her tone turning crafty. "You'll be thirteen at the end of the school year. You promised to return when that happened. Here to the tower, to learn the ways of fairy-tale witches. I'll teach you."

"I can't return," scoffed Rapunzel. "The tower's on Heart Island now."

"I'll move it back when the festival ends," said the witch, taking another step closer.

Rapunzel took a step backward. "How did you move it to the island in the first place? I know your magic isn't strong enough for that."

The witch shrugged. Ducking her head, she kneeled to rip a rampion plant from the patch. She stood again and took a bite of its radishlike root, chomping it raw. "My magic grows stronger every year. And it's already plenty strong enough to cause trouble here for your little friends at the Academy if you don't keep our bargain."

"What kind of trouble?" Rapunzel asked coolly. Recalling what her Handbook had said about the effects of consuming rampion, Rapunzel wondered what the witch's heart's desire was. To see their bargain realized?

"Aha! So you *were* thinking of breaking our bargain." The witch whirled around in a flurry of black robes, then halted and shook a bony finger at her. "Let's make a deal, shall we?"

Typical! thought Rapunzel. The witch couldn't have a single conversation without wheeling and dealing about something. "What deal?"

The witch took another step closer, but then paused, her beady eyes shifting to something beyond Rapunzel.

"You keep your promise to return here at the end of the year, and I'll give you your magical charm."

Rapunzel's brows went up. "Huh? You have my magical charm? I don't believe you."

The witch smiled a secretive smile.

"Show it to me if you really have it," insisted Rapunzel.

"It's in here," the witch told her, pulling a small black bag from inside her cloak. It crackled with magic. From her charm?

Rapunzel's eyes shone as she gazed at the bag. Was her charm really in there? How could the witch have it? She took a step forward. She wanted to open the bag and see. She reached out . . .

But the witch quickly tucked it back inside her cloak. "Return to me as you promised at the year's end, and this charm will be yours. It's worth far more than the treasure those two are hunting." She shifted her gaze over Rapunzel's head.

Rapunzel turned to see two figures in the distance behind her. She craned to see them better as they moved through the trees. Snow and Ms. Wicked! It looked like Ms. Wicked was holding the fake mapestry.

"How did you know they're hunting for treasure?" Rapunzel asked. But when she turned back, the witch was gone. How frustrating! She started to leave, too, but then stopped. Since she was already here, she kneeled to gather handfuls of rampion and put them in her bag. She had a feeling Ms. Queenharts wasn't going to change her mind about the tarts, in which case Hagscorch was going to keep demanding that she gather some of this stuff. So she might as well gather it now.

"What are you doing?" asked a familiar voice. It was Snow.

Rapunzel whipped around. "Um, how long have you been standing there?"

"Long enough to see that witch you were talking to disappear. I saw you both through the trees," said Snow. "Careful," she cautioned before Rapunzel could reply. "My stepmom's right behind me."

"Treasure hunting?" whispered Rapunzel.

Snow nodded.

Just then, Ms. Wicked stepped from the trees to join them in the clearing. She frowned suspiciously at Rapunzel. Then she asked almost the same question Snow had. "Rapunzel? What are you doing in Neverwood?"

"Oh, nothing much," she replied. Thinking fast, she added, "I saw you and Snow come this way, so I followed. What are you guys doing?" She peered curiously at the fashionable handbag Ms. Wicked clutched, figuring it held the fake mapestry and hoping to make the teacher too nervous to ask more questions. Her ploy worked.

"Not a thing," Ms. Wicked replied, crossing her arms

over her bag. "I suppose we should end our stroll and escort Rapunzel back to school," she said to Snow. She sounded a little irritated that her treasure hunt had been interrupted.

"No — you stay and keep, um, enjoying your walk through the woods," Snow told her stepmom. "I'll go back to the island with her."

When Ms. Wicked eagerly agreed to the idea, the girls headed for the Once Upon River. "So?" Snow prompted as they made their way through the trees.

"Okay, you're right. That was a witch I was talking to. Obviously."

"The one who raised you?" Snow guessed.

Rapunzel nodded. They'd reached the river's shore. As they climbed into the two-seater swan boat she had arrived in, she noticed two other identical small swan boats docked farther down the shore. One was probably Ms. Wicked's, but who had brought the other one?

"Is she a good witch?" Snow asked as they launched.

Rapunzel shot Snow an *Are you kidding?* look. "Uh, no. Haven't you read my fairy tale?"

"Well, yes. I mean, sure, I've read it. I know she kept you locked in a tower," Snow said as they paddled back to the island. "But even though the Grimm brothers took great pains to tell everyone's story correctly, they still could've gotten things wrong. So —"

"They got my tale right," Rapunzel interrupted. "The tower I grew up in was in that rampion patch back there. But the witch magicked it over to Heart Island last night. She's up to something."

Snow gasped. She stopped paddling for a minute. "Do you think by any chance . . . that your witch could be the . . . *leader*?"

"As in the leader of E.V.I.L.?" Rapunzel said in surprise. She stopped, too, and they drifted with the current for a time.

Snow nodded. "Moving a tall stone tower from the forest to Heart Island would take powerful magic. The kind E.V.I.L.'s leader probably has. Maybe the witch and the leader are one in the same."

Rapunzel and her friends believed that the society's leader lurked outside the magical wall around Grimmlandia and was somehow guiding E.V.I.L. members in the artifact thefts. So far, only Snow and Cinda had gotten a partial look at this leader, who'd magically appeared to them and then disappeared within a strange mist. A mist that tended to pop up in unexpected places to terrify them.

"I don't think so," Rapunzel said, shaking her head. "My witch lives in Neverwood, not outside the wall. And her magic is strong, but it would take *super*-strong magic to steal artifacts or move a tower. I don't think she could do it by herself. She paused, thinking. "I guess the Society's leader could be helping her, though."

"Yeah, maybe she's part of E.V.I.L. Maybe she made some sort of dastardly deal to help the Society take over the Academy," said Snow. "And all of Grimmlandia, too. You know how witches are, always making wicked deals and bargains."

Yes, Rapunzel did know! A silence fell as both of them began paddling again, thinking their own separate thoughts.

As they neared shore, words burst from Rapunzel, cutting through the quiet. "I did something really stupid. Back when I was six years old, I made a bargain with the witch that I would return to live in the tower and help her with magic the year I turn thirteen."

"What?" said Snow. "But you'll turn thirteen at the end of this year!"

"I know," Rapunzel said miserably. "At the time it seemed like a good idea. It was the only way she'd agree to let me attend Grimm Academy."

"Well, then, we'll just have to figure a way out of that deal," Snow said firmly. "You belong at GA. It just wouldn't be the same without you."

As they docked on the island and disembarked from the swan boat, Rapunzel sent her a sad smile. "But the witch thinks the tower is where I belong. She thinks I'd make a fine witch. That I'd be good at doing evil." Her voice fell to a fearful whisper. "I'm worried that she could be right." She hadn't planned to ever tell anyone this, but it was as if she couldn't stop the grimmawful truth from pouring out of her.

Snow gaped at her. "What? That's crazy. You can't let her make you doubt your own goodness!" When Rapunzel shrugged and looked away, Snow put a hand on her arm and spoke urgently. "Listen, Ms. Wicked's not my real mom and that witch isn't yours, either. But it wouldn't matter if they *were* our real moms. We don't have to be like them if we don't want to. You're a good person. Don't ever let that witch make you think differently about yourself." She gave Rapunzel a hug.

Rapunzel hugged her back, happy Snow felt that way. But would Red and Cinda and all the other kids at the Academy feel the same? And what would the witch do to them if Rapunzel backed out on her promise? Get really mad, that's what. If she truly was powerful enough to move a tower nowadays, maybe she could also do real harm to GA — even if she wasn't the leader of E.V.I.L.

Just then, Red and Cinda appeared on the dock. "Don't tell them what we talked about, okay?" Rapunzel cautioned Snow all in a rush. "It's kind of embarrassing for me. I want to try to solve my witch problem on my own before telling them anything."

"Okay," Snow promised uncertainly. "But I'm sure they'd want to help. I mean, they're our friends. "

True, but Rapunzel didn't want to take the risk that they might pull away from their friendship with her if they found out the things she'd kept hidden.

When Red and Cinda reached them, Red wrapped her cape close and hopped into a swan boat big enough to seat four. "Ready to go?" she asked the other three girls. She and Cinda didn't seem to have a clue that Rapunzel and Snow had ever gone off-island, or that they had only just returned from Neverwood.

Snow and Rapunzel didn't bother telling them otherwise. Instead, they simply joined the other two girls in the boat and shoved off.

"We were thinking we should have a dinnertime picnic in Rapunzel's room tonight," said Red, as they began to paddle toward school. "What do you say?" That began a discussion of what to eat, and about the day's events.

Once they'd docked at the drawbridge outside Grimm Academy, the girls headed to the Great Hall kitchen for picnic supplies. While Snow, Red, and Cinda fetched food from cabinets, Rapunzel darted over to Hagscorch's icebox. She pulled out some berries for their picnic, and replaced them with the rampion stalks she'd pulled from the witch's garden. Then she slammed the icebox door shut again. Good riddance!

Later, once she and her friends had finished eating in her dungeon room, they all sat on her bed and talked for hours. About normal stuff, like the gowns they planned to check out of the Grimmstone Library the next day for the Festival Ball and about charms, crushes, and classes, too.

Eventually, Red yawned and asked, "Whose turn is it to keep the mapestry?"

"Snow's, I think," said Cinda, as she and the other two Grimm girls prepared to leave.

Snow shook her head doubtfully. "I don't think I should take it. While I'm pretend-helping my stepmom hunt for treasure, she might snoop in my bag or something. She's done that before. Besides, she sometimes gives me the fake mapestry to carry and I wouldn't want to get the two mixed up."

"I'll keep it," Rapunzel offered, and everyone nodded. So when the others left for Pearl Tower, she looked for a place in her room to hide the mapestry. There was a deep, narrow empty space where a stone was missing from the wall by her bed. She set the mapestry far back in the space and whispered a chant she'd learned in Bespellings and Enchantments class.

Dungeon wall of granite stone,
Keep this hiding place unknown.

There was a grinding sound, like rock sliding across rock. A stone magically appeared to cover the entrance to the hole in the wall, disguising the location of the mapestry.

The deed done, Rapunzel threw off her clothes and put on her nightgown. Then she snuggled under her comforter. For a while, she tossed and turned. It was hard to get to sleep knowing that in just two more days the E.V.I.L. Society planned to take over the Academy! Exhausted, she eventually put her worries to bed and was able to drift off.

6

Deals and Threads

The next morning, Rapunzel woke to the sound of voices. It was the GA School Board making morning announcements from where they sat upon their carved wooden shelf on the Great Hall's west balcony.

"Good morning, scholars!" the helmet heads chorused. "Breakfast will be served in the Great Hall in precisely one half hour." Even though she couldn't see them, she could hear the soft *creak, creak* of those five shiny helmets' visors opening and closing as they spoke. Their voices continued on, piped throughout the school via a complicated system that involved magical tubes. "Afternoon classes have been canceled by order of the great and goodly principal of Grimm Academy so that all festival preparations may be finalized on Heart Island. We bid you all a good Friday!"

Rapunzel pushed off her thick, warm comforter and hopped out of bed, her bare feet sinking into the plush black-and-white checkered rug on her floor. The four cats who'd been snuggled on the bed with her hopped out, too.

Mordred was more a loner than the others and had slept high on the windowsill. But now he jumped down to follow her around.

If she had to go live with the witch again, what would happen to her cats? she worried. She couldn't take them to the tower with her. She didn't trust the witch not to try to turn them evil, which was exactly what she hoped to do to Rapunzel, of course. Well, she wasn't going to let either of those things happen. There had to be some way to free herself from their deal!

She padded over to her desk and armoire. There, she got some food for her cats from the small icebox and filled their bowls with fresh water from the pump, which also fed her shower. That was one nice thing about having your own room. The dorm girls all shared, but she had a private bathroom.

In fact, for a dungeon, her room was really cute — in a goth kind of way. Black lacy curtains hung from the window over her bed, and tasseled black, gray, and white pillows of various shapes and sizes were scattered about the room. One of them even had twelve sparkly jet-black jewels sewn onto it — a gift from Snow on her last birthday.

Quickly, Rapunzel donned a scoop-necked long black dress that was patterned with tiny dark-gray polka dots. She added leggings and chunky-heel ankle boots. Although her hair was behaving at the moment, she wasn't taking any chances. She wove it into six braids, and then wove those together into one long braid at her back. Lastly, she put on a pair of silver half-moon earrings.

By the time she was dressed for morning classes, four of her cats had snuggled back on her bed, and Mordred was again snoozing on the windowsill. She bid them all a soft farewell, headed for breakfast and then, afterward, for her first-period Sieges, Catapults, and Jousts class.

Four days a week, the class was held out on the lawn by Gray Castle. But Fridays were indoor studies. And this morning — surprise! Someone new stood at the front of the classroom instead of her usual teacher. His smile was blinding white, and he had a straight, sharp-pointed mustache. It jutted out about four inches on either side of his face, and ended in curlicues in front of his ears.

"Who's that?" Basil asked, nodding toward the unfamiliar teacher as he took a seat next to Rapunzel. Most students in this class were boys.

"Substitute, I think," she replied.

"What a fine-looking class you are!" said the new teacher. "Coach Candlestick is busy at the festival grounds this morning and asked me to step in for him." He whipped off his top hat to reveal hair that was slicked down from a center part, and took a bow. "My name is Mr. Dickory. Of Barter, Bargain, Dicker, and Deal Auctions and Estate Sales," he added when he straightened again. Then he promptly passed out his business cards to everyone. "We represent clients from fairy tales, folk tales, and nursery rhymes. I'm sure you've heard of our company."

Rapunzel nodded. Everyone at GA knew of Mr. Dickory and his cousin Mr. Hickory, who'd founded their company together. They were famous for having made many excellent deals, including one to buy a grandfather clock, which they'd then donated to the Academy. It was the very clock that now stood in the Great Hall and was called Hickory Dickory in their honor. A generous donation as well as good advertising for them.

Mr. Dickory rubbed his hands together eagerly. "I don't know much about sieges, so today, we are going to talk about bad bargains in nursery rhymes. I know this isn't the usual subject matter for this class, but I think you'll find it interesting just the same. Now! Can someone name such a bad bargain?"

Students began offering suggestions. "Jack traded a cow for beans that grew a beanstalk," said Basil.

Yes, that was sort of like what her mom had done, thought Rapunzel. Only she'd traded *her own daughter* to get rampion!

She was usually pretty quiet in class. But now she sat up straight and her hand shot into the air. This could be her chance to get some advice on how to weasel out of her bargain with the witch, she realized. But she'd have to couch her question carefully so as not to reveal her personal interest in the matter.

"Could Jack have somehow gotten out of that deal? I mean, after he discovered he'd made a bad one?" she asked when called on.

"Interesting question," said Mr. Dickory, pacing back and forth at the front of the room. "Some bargains are fair and square. Fifty-fifty deals. In others, there's a winner and a loser. In either case, once a deal is made, it's final. Therefore, Jack was stuck." He paused, then added, "However, if my company had been representing him as our client, we would have looked for a loophole. Or some way to strike a new, second deal. One that was more favorable to him."

As Rapunzel considered that information, the teacher went on with his lesson.

"There are five deal-making Dos," he announced. "You can apply them to your own deals in the future. But for now, we'll pretend we're advising Jack."

He held up one finger. "Number One! When offered the magic beans, you should appear interested in them, but not *too* interested.

"Number Two! Talk about what you don't like about the beans — maybe they're too brown. Or somewhat wrinkled. Don't be rude. Just sound unsure.

"Number Three! Wait silently. The bean seller will get nervous that you'll back out. He might offer a better deal."

Boing! Just then, a strand of hair popped straight up from Mr. Dickory's head. He licked the palm of his hand and patted the hair down, smoothing it back.

"Maybe you should try that with your hair if it starts —" Basil began.

"Don't!" Rapunzel whispered frantically. "Don't say that *W* word that rhymes with *jiggle*. It'll make my hair start w-i-g-g-l-you-know-what-ing again."

Basil grinned and whispered back, "Got it." Pressing his thumb and fingertip together at one side of his mouth, he zipped them across his lips.

"Number Four!" Mr. Dickory was saying. "Ask the bean seller to work with you on the deal. Smile and be friendly. But don't beg.

"Number Five! Walk away. Don't be afraid to leave a bad deal. Often, the bean seller will call you back and suggest a better one."

By the time class was over, Rapunzel was excited. She felt she'd just been handed a set of tools to do a job. Like a carpenter who'd been given a hammer, nails, and a saw to build a house. Although she wasn't exactly thrilled about the prospect of meeting up with the witch again, she did feel better prepared.

In her next period Threads class, she sat with Snow. As they worked on stitching samplers, Rapunzel thought some more about Mr. Dickory's suggestions. Next time she saw the witch, would she be able to put them into practice?

"This probably seems like it's coming out of the blue, but I've been thinking about your fear of heights," Snow said, cutting through her thoughts. "I wonder if it might help to talk to people who work at jobs that are high up, and ask them how they keep calm?"

"Maybe like the tower window washers, you mean?" Rapunzel asked.

Snow nodded. "Or even Jack and Jill. They're always climbing hills — some even as tall as mountains — and it doesn't seem to bother them."

Rapunzel nodded. "I guess it's worth a shot. Anyway, thanks for trying to help." She sent Snow a smile and Snow smiled back. It was nice to know that she hadn't been put off their friendship after learning of Rapunzel's deepest fear that she might become an evil witch.

She looked over from her own uneven stitchery to study Snow's neat sampler. There was an embroidered illustration of Grimm Academy in the middle of it. Around the border, Snow had stitched the ABCs. *Hmm. The alphabet.* Something tugged at Rapunzel's brain.

"What's wrong?" asked Snow, noticing her frown. She turned her sampler to gaze at it. "Did I miss a stitch? Or forget a letter?"

"No, your work is perfect, as usual," Rapunzel soothed. "Sorry for staring. I just spaced out while thinking of something else, that's all. I —"

"No! Stop it!" two voices interrupted.

"What?" Startled, Rapunzel whipped around. *Oh no!* Her hair had escaped its braid again. It had wiggled out and tangled itself in the yellow sock Goldilocks was knitting and in the pink, flower-shaped hat Mary Mary Quite Contrary was crocheting.

"Sorry!" said Rapunzel. "Did one of you just say the word w-i-g-g-l-e?"

"I did, I guess," said Goldilocks. "Because my yarn was sort of wiggling around. Why?"

"Never mind," said Snow. Rapunzel sighed as the four girls promptly got busy untangling her long, black hair from the yarn.

"Want to use my comb to redo your hair?" Mary Mary offered once they'd finished the job.

Rapunzel smiled slightly. "That's okay. I have my own." She fished around for it in her black bag.

"Here, really, use mine," Mary Mary coaxed. When Rapunzel automatically started to refuse, Mary Mary looked upset. "You're still mad about Bespellings class, aren't you? I didn't mean to sneeze that tongue twister spell on your hair, you know."

"I'm not mad," Rapunzel said honestly. "I know you didn't do it on purpose."

"Then why not use my comb?" Mary Mary pouted. The contrary girl seemed oddly determined. Which was a little suspicious. Why did she care if anyone borrowed her comb or not?

Rapunzel rolled her eyes a little, so only Snow could see. Then she turned to Mary Mary and held out her hand. "Okay, thanks."

When the girl set the onyx comb in her palm, Rapunzel gazed at it in wonder. It was a deep, rich, polished black and its spine was carved with fanciful wild plants.

"Wow, that's beautiful," Snow commented.

Rapunzel felt Mary Mary watching her. "It really is," she told the girl. It felt so right in her hand. Its teeth didn't catch at all as she used it to work out her tangles. "Where did you get it? I'd love to have one like it."

"I, um, found it," said Mary Mary quickly. "So does your hair feel any different?"

"Well, your comb got the tangles out," said Rapunzel, unsure why she was asking. With Snow's help (and the comb's), she quickly rebraided her hair.

"Oh." Mary Mary heaved a disappointed sigh. Then, as the clock sounded the end of the period, she abruptly snatched the comb back and dashed off. Rapunzel gazed

after her, feeling a sense of loss. And a strange sort of long-
ing for that comb.

"So we'll all be meeting in the library before lunch?"
said Snow, drawing her attention. "To choose ball gowns?"

"Right. See you then," said Rapunzel, nodding.

Fridays in her third-period Bespellings were a free day
to practice spells, catch up on homework, or do a magic-
related service around the school. Since she had chosen to
help in the library, it would be easy to meet her friends
there and get gowns before going to lunch.

"Start thinking sparkles," Snow advised with a smile.
"For your gown, I mean." Snow loved embellishing her
clothes with ribbons, sparkles, and gems, and she was
always trying to get Rapunzel and the other girls to do the
same with their gowns.

Rapunzel grinned back. "I will. Promise." She put away
her stitchery, then they both headed out of the classroom
along with everyone else. Immediately, Rapunzel began
searching the hall for a certain doorknob. One that would
admit her to the library.

The Academy's Grimmstone Library was an amazing
place that held not only books but also boxes of weird
things such as kisses, bubbles, and boasts. Not to mention
artifacts like Hush-a-bye Baby's cradle and Little Boy Blue's
horn. Rapunzel and her BFFs especially loved the aisles
where you could find the gowns and dancing slippers,

which students could check out and wear whenever there was a ball.

The only problem with the library was that it was impossible to know where it might be on any given day. It moved around the Academy and you had to find the special doorknob — the only one without the GA logo on it — to locate its entrance.

"Gotcha!" Rapunzel felt lucky to spot the knob in the very first place she looked — on a wall along the second floor of Pink Castle, right down the hall from Threads class.

Honk! The plain brass knob morphed into the shape of a beaked goose's head the moment she touched it.

She shifted from one foot to the other, waiting. Students always had to answer a riddle before the gooseknob would admit them to the library. When the knob said no more, she prompted, "Well? May I have a riddle, please?"

"Wait just a knob-honking minute!" the beaky knob grouched. "Do you think doorknobs just sit around thinking up riddles all day so we can be ready for visitors?"

Actually, Rapunzel had never given a thought to what doorknobs did or didn't do when no one was turning them. But surely this one wasn't so busy that it couldn't think up and stockpile enough riddles to be ready when someone did turn it.

"Answer me this!" the gooseknob said at last. "What kind of glances lead upward?"

Rapunzel's head jerked back. *Huh?* Why had the gooseknob chosen to ask her a riddle about going *up*? Was it possible it knew about her fear of stairs? Like just about everyone else at this school did? Hey! That gave her an idea for the answer.

"Stairs?" she guessed. "The kind you walk up. Which sounds the same as *stares*, as in staring or glancing at someone."

Snick! Without another word, the gooseknob magically turned back into a plain brass knob again. That was how you knew you'd guessed the riddle correctly. Quickly, a rectangular door drew itself on the wall around the knob. It was several feet taller than Rapunzel and about four feet wide, decorated with low-relief carvings of nursery-rhyme characters such as Little Bo Peep and her sheep. Rapunzel turned the knob.

7

Missing Artifacts

Rapunzel stepped inside the library and glanced around, unsure exactly what she'd find. Because another unusual thing about this place was that it could change its shape from wardrobe-size to enormous. It was enormous today — as tall as the witch's tower and almost as vast as Neverwood Forest.

Flap! Flap! Suddenly, two snow-white geese zoomed right over her head. There were dozens of them flying high above, carrying books and artifacts hither and thither in nets that hung from their orange beaks. She waved to them on her way in.

Her footsteps echoed in the entryway as she crossed to stand before a tall desk. There was a bell, a gooseneck lamp, and a basket full of goose-feather quill pens on top of it. Beyond the desk, stretching so far into the distance that she could see no end to them, were row after row of shelves. And rooms, too, filled with who knew what. Some housed special collections, like the Grimm brothers' room, which was the most magical place in the library. Probably in all of Grimmlandia!

"Ms. Goose?" Rapunzel picked up the bell and rang it. When the librarian didn't appear, she ventured beyond the desk.

Whoosh! A flying goose that was much larger than all the rest, swooped down toward her. Rapunzel ducked as it landed nearby. The woman riding the horse-size goose hopped off and approached her. She wore a frilly white cap and spectacles, and her crisp white apron had a curlicue *L* embroidered on its front bib. *L* for Librarian.

"Hi, Ms. Goose," said Rapunzel.

Ms. Goose smiled and gave her a quick hug. As usual, she smelled like a combination of peppermints, face powder, and cleverness. "Goodness, is it Friday already?" she said. "Well, let's see what needs doing around here today, shall we?"

The librarian went over to the desk and riffled through a large box labeled THINGS THAT NEED DOING. She pulled a feather from it and stared at it in puzzlement. Then she brightened. "Yes, I remember now. This is from Mr. Wildswan's wing. To remind me he needs an object for Monday's class on morphing." Mr. Wildswan, who had one normal arm and one that was a swan's wing, taught Shape-Shifting at the Academy.

Ms. Goose put the reminder feather back into the box and pulled out a pumpkin seed. After examining it for a second, she said, "Oh, and Peter Peter would like something to replace his missing pumpkin since it went over the wall."

Rapunzel cocked her head in question. "You mean like a giant turnip or watermelon?"

"Good ideas. However, he said he'd prefer something that begins with the letter *P*," said Ms. Goose.

"Perhaps a prodigious pickle?" Rapunzel suggested with a grin.

"I'll leave the choice to you," Ms. Goose replied, smiling at her silly alliteration. "Want me to fly you around while you do these assignments, dear?"

"No, thanks," said Rapunzel. Ms. Goose always seemed to forget that she had a fear of heights. She'd *never* flown on the big white goose. The idea of swooping up to the library ceiling was enough to make her swoon — if she ever swooned, that is.

Just then, Rapunzel remembered Snow's suggestion to ask questions of people who worked in high places. "What's it like to fly so high?" she asked the librarian.

"Ooh, it used to scare me, zooming around this place," Ms. Goose admitted, pushing her glasses higher on her nose. "But walking takes altogether too long. In my early days, before I flew, it sometimes took me a whole day to get from one end of the library to the other. I'd have to sleep at the far end and walk back to the entrance the next day. By flying, I get more done. Besides, a goose-eye view of the library helps me notice when items are missing."

"You mean, as in missing books?"

Ms. Goose nodded. "And artifacts as well. Which reminds me." She handed Rapunzel a net bag containing an antique-looking xylophone about twelve inches long. "This artifact should be replaced in the Grimm brothers' room for safekeeping. It belongs to one of the Bremen musicians."

Rapunzel knew why she was being asked to do this instead of the geese. It was because, for some reason, they refused to enter the Grimm brothers' room. Which meant that items going to and from that room had to be hand delivered by Ms. Goose herself or by student helpers.

Ms. Goose went on. "And while you're in there" — she turned away to check a note in her THINGS THAT NEED DOING box — "please alphabetize the file cards you'll find on the Grimm brothers' desk." She bent to tuck her box under her desk. "Now we'd better both get a wiggle on. There's much to do!"

Whap! While the librarian's back was still turned, a lock of Rapunzel's long hair suddenly wriggled loose from her braid and whipped out to wrap itself around the xylophone. Rapunzel yanked her tresses free and tucked them back into place before they drew Ms. Goose's notice. *Crazy hair!* It had responded to the word *wiggle,* of course.

"I'm on it," Rapunzel assured the librarian. Saying a quick farewell, she zipped off to the *S* section first. She absolutely loved this library. It had so many cozy corners and intriguing, forgotten objects.

Pausing before a shelf full of shape-shifting objects in the main part of the library, she selected a silver tiara that kept morphing into a silk top hat and then back again into a tiara. It seemed perfect for Mr. Wildswan's needs. She held the tiara-top-hat high above her head. Immediately, a goose with an empty net swooped down and hauled it away.

As the goose flew back toward the librarian's desk, Rapunzel thought she felt a lock of her hair dart toward some shells sitting on a shelf across from where she'd found the shape-shifting tiara-top-hat. But when she patted her head and then tugged her braid forward over one shoulder to examine it, she discovered that every hair was in place As were the shells on the shelf. Her hair had stolen things in the Great Hall. However, in here it seemed only to be *touching* various items but not actually stealing them. That was an improvement anyway, she supposed. Strange, though.

She examined the shells her hair had touched and saw that they were Mary Mary Quite Contrary's. Rumor had it that these cockleshells were both her charm and an artifact, and that they were also what caused her con-trariness. Since they were here, she must've loaned them to the library, which students did from time to time for safekeeping.

While she was still in the *S* aisle, Rapunzel spotted a shelf labeled SPELL BOOKS. Two of the titles were *Smelly Spells* and *Spells to Foil Fairy-Tale Crooks*. Setting down the net bag with the xylophone, she pulled out the first one, then quickly slammed it shut. It stunk like a skunk!

Next, she tried the one about crooks. It contained pun-ishments for all sorts of bad-deed-doers such as witches, trolls, and ogres. There were chapter titles like "How to Trap a Fairy-Tale Crook in a Book" and "How to Hook a Fairy-Tale Crook in a Brook." But ickiest of all was the chap-ter titled "How to Capture and Cook a Fairy-Tale Crook!"

Next, she selected an old leather-bound book with fancy lettering titled *Hairy Spells*. She thumbed to a chapter called "Accidentally Inflicted Snarlies, Twists, or Wiggles" and began reading aloud to herself in a soft voice: " 'These spells will eventually untangle themselves when the hair affected by the spell grows out. However, under no cir-cumstances should bespelled hair be cut within the first twenty-four hours after the spell is cast.' "

Or what? she wondered. The book didn't say. Still, maybe it was a good thing she hadn't shaved it off like Snow had half-jokingly suggested! It was a relief to learn that the wiggles must be like hair dye, and would grow out as time passed.

"Surprise and salutations!" called a voice. Startled, Rapunzel jumped and swung around, snapping the book shut. Meanwhile, Cinda poked her head around the far end of the shelf and grinned at her.

"Yikes, you scared me. What are you doing here so soon?" asked Rapunzel. "Third period has barely started."

"Sorry about that. The greeting seemed appropriate since we're in the *S* section," Cinda said, stepping into the aisle to join her. "Mr. Dickory canceled third-period Sieges and Catapults. An emergency estate sale he had to get to. I figured I'd come be your assistant till Red and Snow show up to hunt for gowns with us before lunch."

"Grimmtastic," Rapunzel said, smiling now.

Cinda bowed her head, pretending to be a servant. "I am at your command. So what can I do?"

Rapunzel slid the spell book she was holding back into place on the shelf and picked up the xylophone, at the same time explaining the jobs Ms. Goose had asked her to do. "I already got the shape-shifting object. Now we need find something to replace Peter Peter's missing pumpkin."

Cinda pointed to a large squash. "This squash seems suitable," she said, using more *S* words.

Rapunzel grinned. "It's sizable!" she agreed. "And since Peter Peter's a magician, he could make it bigger or smaller whenever he needs to, like he could his pumpkin. However, he requested a *P* object."

"Poor Peter," said Cinda, sighing as they both headed for the *P* section. "Losing his pumpkin artifact over the wall."

Rapunzel nodded. "You know, I've wondered why his artifact was the first one stolen." Since then, others had gone missing. Just a couple of weeks ago, the Pied Piper's pipe had tried to lead even more artifacts away by piping a tune that some of the items had followed. Luckily, Snow had foiled that theft.

The girls discussed the matter as they moved through the *R* and *Q* sections, heading back toward the *P*s. Twice along the way, Rapunzel felt a lock of her hair lash out to touch something on a shelf. "Stop that!" she told it each time. Each time it obeyed, unwrapping the object and leaving it in its original place.

When they reached the *P*s they quickly decided on a three-foot-tall pineapple for Peter Peter. "Peter Peter Pineapple Eater," mused Rapunzel. "It has a ring to it — as in *pineapple ring*." The girls giggled. Then, since the pineapple was pretty large and prickly, they waved over two geese to pick it up.

"This place is so grimmmazing," said Cinda as they watched the geese wing the big pineapple back toward Ms. Goose's desk at the library entrance.

Rapunzel felt the same way. The Grimm brothers had brought everything here that they believed needed protection. Pieces of music, the fountain of youth, irreplaceable documents, fantastical rooms, enchanted artifacts, mysterious memories. The library held collections beyond anything a person could imagine or explore in a whole lifetime.

"Yeah," she replied. "But if you ask Ms. Goose how a library this big fits inside the Academy, she'll only say . . ."

Both girls spoke the librarian's familiar response: "It's magical. Movable. Timeless. Formless." Then they laughed.

"As if that explains everything," said Rapunzel. "Actually, Grimmstone is more a cross between a library and a museum, don't you think? Maybe it should be renamed the Grimmstone Libseum."

"Or the Grimmstone Muserary," said Cinda. Which cracked them both up again. "What's next?" she asked when they'd finally managed to stop laughing.

Rapunzel held up the orange net bag containing the xylophone. "We need to return this to the Grimm brothers' room. Are you okay with that?" she asked, a little concerned for her friend.

On Cinda's very first day at GA, in that very room, she had seen someone peeking at her through a coat of arms. Which had scared her silly!

The girls now suspected it might have been the leader

of the E.V.I.L. Society. Snow had seen the very same face appear later in the doorknob of Ms. Wicked's classroom.

Cinda nodded. "I've wanted to go back there, and it'll be easier with a friend. Hopefully, no eyeballs will spy on us this time, though." She shuddered.

A few turns later, they stepped across the threshold of the Grimm brothers' room, where Jacob and Wilhelm had once penned their fairy tales. They'd brought this entire room and its contents here from its original location so it could be preserved and kept safe forever.

Dozens of portraits hung on one of its walls, including seven in carved golden frames that were grouped together in the center. For some reason, one of those seven was covered with a drape, so the painting it held couldn't be seen.

Around the portraits and elsewhere along the walls, the polished bookshelves were stuffed with things belonging to the Grimm brothers. A sign on one shelf read:

Protected here are the writings of the
Grimm brothers, Charles Perrault,
Hans Christian Andersen, L. Frank Baum,
Lewis Carroll, Andrew Lang, Edmund Dulac,
Mother Goose, and other great works of
fairy tale, folklore, and nursery rhyme.

"What'll happen to this room if the Society gets its way? If E.V.I.L.'s leader takes over the Academy?" Cinda wondered aloud. "We can't forget what Ms. Wicked's datebook said they have planned for Monday." She pitched her voice to sound evil. "GA is ours!"

Rapunzel shivered. "We'll stop them. Somehow. We have to!"

All around them, objects were moving about the room under their own power. A pair of shiny red patent leather shoes over in one corner were dancing to music the girls couldn't hear. A bunch of checkers were slowly and aimlessly floating around like black and red snowflakes.

A feather pen kept dipping itself in a bottle of ink that sat on the huge, ornate desk. Above the desk hung the Grimm brothers' splendid coat of arms, which looked like a big shield with various gold emblems on it. Cinda and Rapunzel eyed it warily.

"I don't see anything, do you?" Rapunzel whispered. "No eyeballs or noses? No hazy mist?"

"No," Cinda agreed, and they both breathed a sigh of relief.

Just then, a pair of spectacles with round lenses lifted off the desk. They flew over and set themselves on Rapunzel's face. Startled, she reached out to remove them, but they'd already taken themselves off. They flew back to the desk and gradually lowered until they came to rest on it again. Right beside a box of index cards labeled STOLEN ARTIFACTS.

"See if you can figure out where this goes. Ms. Goose said it belongs in here somewhere," said Rapunzel, handing Cinda the xylophone. "While you do that, I'll file those missing artifacts cards on the desk over there in alphabetical order like she asked me to."

After handing Cinda the net bag containing the xylophone, Rapunzel went over and sat down in the big leather desk chair. She opened the file box. To her surprise, there were easily more than a dozen cards inside.

Still holding the bagged xylophone, Cinda came to look over her shoulder at the cards. "Each of those is for an artifact that has gone missing? But I only thought a few had been stolen, beginning this year."

"Me, too," said Rapunzel, thumbing through them. "But there's a missing golden apple, a horn, a jack-in-the-box. I count seventeen things that have disappeared from the library in all." As she began organizing the cards, Cinda went over to a display of musical instruments.

"Oops!" said Cinda. Rapunzel looked over to see that she had almost tripped over a metal wind-up toy hedgehog about eight inches tall that was lumbering around on the floor. Finding a blank space on a shelf of musical instruments just big enough for the xylophone, Cinda carefully set it between a lute, a glockenspiel, and a tambourine, then came back to the desk.

By that time, Rapunzel had alphabetized all seventeen cards. "Look!" she told Cinda, a chill sweeping her. "There's a date on each card, showing when the artifacts went missing. They were stolen in alphabetical order over the last six years."

The girls stared at each other. "What could it mean?" asked Cinda. Then her eyes shifted upward. She sucked in a sharp breath and began backing away from the desk.

Rapunzel followed her gaze to the coat of arms hanging on the wall. As she stared at the shield within the coat of arms, something changed. All at once, a small, roundish area of the shield went misty and foggy. Transparent, almost! And then . . . what was that . . . was there a nose showing through? She jumped up and hugged Cinda. Together they stood shivering, too mesmerized to unglue their gaze from the coat of arms.

"It's happening again," Cinda whispered in a scared voice.

"I know," whispered Rapunzel. Slowly, they began backing toward the door.

Suddenly, a hand reached out of the coat of arms, then an actual *arm*. "The . . . *X* . . . too," an ancient voice whispered.

"Ahhh!" Both girls shrieked. They took off at a run. Rapunzel hopped over the wind-up hedgehog on her way out. They ran all the way to the *G* section, where they came upon Red and Snow waiting for them to start gown shopping. Breathlessly, they told them what had happened and about the seventeen objects that had been stolen in ABC order.

Snow gasped. "That makes so much sense! When I captured the Pied Piper's pipe, it had collected a trail of six artifacts. In line order, they were a chess piece, a ruby ring, the spoon and silver dish, a man's tie, an umbrella, and a vase. See what I mean? They were in alphabetical order after the *P* for Peter Peter's pumpkin: *Q R S T U V*!"

"Chess piece is a *C*, though, not a *Q*," Cinda commented.

"But it was the white *queen* piece, remember?" Snow countered. "A *Q* artifact."

"I guess E.V.I.L. must've already collected *A* through *O* before we even noticed them stealing artifacts," Red noted.

"There's something I don't get. The last two object cards in the file box were the pail and the pumpkin," said Rapunzel. "Why do you think two *P*s were stolen?"

"Maybe my stepsisters duplicated the *P* theft by accident, trying to score points with the Society by stealing the pumpkin," suggested Cinda. "Maybe meanwhile, someone else was already plotting to steal the pail to stall Principal R's alchemy experiments instead?"

"Yeah, who knows? But since Snow foiled E.V.I.L.'s attempt to use the Pied Piper's pipe to steal more artifacts, I'm guessing they'll be trying again. Starting over with *Q*."

"The real question is, why is E.V.I.L. trying to steal artifacts in alphabetical order at all?" asked Rapunzel. Then her breath caught as an answer came to her. "Maybe once they have artifacts *A* through *Z*, the spell protecting the wall around Grimmlandia will be weakened enough that their leader can break through it!"

The other three Grimm girls stared at her. "Oh, no," whispered Cinda.

"Should we tell someone? Ms. Goose? Principal R?" Snow asked uncertainly.

"The Enchantress!" said Red. Grandmother Enchantress was one of the most ancient and powerful people in the entire realm. A sister to the Grimm brothers, she was also Wolfgang's great-great-grandmother. She sometimes appeared to the girls in a special crystal ball that he'd recently hidden in the library's Crystal Room.

Rapunzel and her friends ran there, only to have their hopes dashed. Though they searched high and low among small crystal animals like unicorns and big crystal chandeliers and candelabras, they didn't find the Enchantress's crystal ball.

"What now?" asked Red.

"We agreed not to trust anyone with what we know,"

said Rapunzel. "I say we keep it that way. Because if we accidentally tip off someone in the E.V.I.L. Society, there's no telling what'll happen."

"Agreed," said Cinda. "So let's just pick out our gowns and slippers, and then take the mapestry to the island again like we planned."

The Grimm girls quickly chose slippers and gowns for the ball and tagged them to pick up later. Afterward, Rapunzel got the mapestry from her wall hiding place and met Snow, Cinda, and Red by the swan boats at the drawbridge. Together, they sailed over to Heart Island in hopes of finding riches to save the school and defeat E.V.I.L. Before the Monday deadline hinted at on Ms. Wicked's calendar!

But after hours of searching the heart-shaped fountains on the back lawn, the croquet field, and the picnic area near the gazebos, they were back at the Academy again, disappointed and tired. They still hadn't found any treasure. If the festival didn't earn enough money, what would happen to their beloved school? Was it doomed to be closed and turned evil in just two more days?

8

Fair Day!

It was Saturday, the day of the festival. Despite not having found the treasure, and despite the upheaval of the last few days, Rapunzel was excited. She and her friends had planned and worked so hard on this event. She really hoped it would be a success!

"Come on, Mordred!" she called. She grabbed her black bag, which was full of prize ribbons for the pet show. The cat followed her out of the Academy as she went to meet her three Grimm girl friends in the Bouquet Garden so they could all go to Heart Island together. Plus, they'd agreed to help transport some additional bouquets Mary Mary Quite Contrary had picked to decorate the island's amphitheater.

An extraordinary variety of flowers grew in the garden — roses, tulips, lilies, daisies, carnations, orchids, and dozens more. Unlike most flowers, however, these actually bloomed in ready-made assorted-flower bouquets.

Red, Snow, Cinda, and Mary Mary were already setting

bouquets in carts when Rapunzel arrived in the garden. Mordred chased butterflies while they worked.

"Got the *You Know What*?" Rapunzel quietly asked Red as they wheeled the flower-filled carts down to the swan-shaped boats docked alongside the Once Upon River. She'd given her the mapestry the night before. Red nodded and patted the basket she carried. If there was time, they'd treasure hunt again today.

Mordred followed the girls and leaped into one of the boats, sitting in Rapunzel's lap on the way over to the festival grounds. They had to take two of the larger boats so they could carry all the flowers. Mary Mary followed in a third, smaller boat.

As they docked on Heart Island, Mordred wriggled in Rapunzel's arms. She set him down on shore. "You can run around, but check in with me now and then, okay?" she told him.

Mrrr, Mordred agreed. Then he leaped away, off to investigate.

"Isn't this grimmnificent?" said Red as they passed others helping with last-minute setup along the path. "So many people volunteered to help. I just hope we get a big turnout."

The potted tongue twister plants from all of Ms. Blue Fairygodmother's Bespellings and Enchantments classes had been set here and there around the festival grounds, Rapunzel noticed. She was too busy to stop and admire them, though, as the girls rushed the carts to the amphitheater. There, they placed the bouquets where Mary Mary wanted them, at intervals along the two main seating aisles and across the front of the stage.

Not long afterward, crowds of people from all over Grimmlandia started to arrive. And soon two musicians appeared onstage and raised their long, thin, golden herald trumpets to their lips. *Ta-ta-ta-ta-ta-ta-tum!* blared the trumpets. At the sound, most everyone on the island headed for the amphitheater. Having gotten their attention, the musicians lowered their instruments and waited as people gathered in the theater seats and grew quiet.

"Attention, scholars and citizens!" they chorused a few minutes later. "All hail the principal of Grimm Academy." It was time for the festival to officially begin!

The red velvet curtains behind the musicians whipped open just wide enough for the principal to step out from behind them. The rear of the stage was decorated with the sets and backdrops for Red and Wolfgang's dramatic play tonight, but all that was hidden beyond the curtains for now.

Stomp! Stomp! Stomp! Principal Rumpelstiltskin, who was a gnome and three feet tall at most, walked up to a podium, where he climbed a small stepstool to make himself appear at least somewhat taller before the assembled crowd. Rapunzel hoped no one would accidently address him by his real name. Seeing him throw a fit would definitely start the festival off on the wrong foot!

The diminutive principal spread his arms wide, appearing to be in high spirits for once. "Good morning, people of Grimmlandia. What a perfect day for our festival!"

Everyone cheered his remark. When the applause died down, he continued. "Please enjoy the rides! Gobble goodies at the food gazebos! Play games! See the pet show! Vote for your favorite tongue twister plant! However," he said, leaning forward, "at the same time, be on the lookout for any unusual activity." He didn't say what that unusual activity might be, but Rapunzel was sure he meant signs of artifacts being stolen.

Now the principal turned and stomped back down his stepstool. A wary hush had fallen over the crowd at the vague warning contained in his last words.

Stomp! Stomp! Stomp! Seeming to realize he'd put a damper on things, he came back up to the podium, a huge grin on his face now. "And have a happily-ever-after day at the festival, one and all!"

At that, there was more cheering and clapping. Then everyone took off in different directions to enjoy the festival.

"Let's do the catapults first," Cinda urged the other three Grimm girls, nudging them toward the great lawn where Coach Candlestick was directing the competition. She loved most sports and was really good at them.

Mr. Hump-Dumpty was standing on the sidelines of the lawn, shouting advice to the students who were competing with huge battering rams, catapults, and other siege engines. When the girls took their turns lobbing hay bales from catapults, he called out to them, "Be careful!" "Watch out!" "Oh, that looks very dangerous!"

Typical! thought Rapunzel. He was the biggest worrywart at the Academy.

She, Snow, and Red clapped and whooped when Cinda catapulted a bale all the way out to the middle of the Once Upon River. That was farther than any of the others girls and boys had managed so far.

Next, Rapunzel and her BFFs decided to roll down Jack and Jill Hill inside Ms. Blue Fairygodmother's big, magical bubbles. Snow chose a turquoise one, Red a red one, while Cinda went with pink, and Rapunzel chose a silver one. The roll downhill was wild, dizzying, hilarious fun!

"I'm going to try my luck at cruel-heart darts," Snow said after the rides. "If your dart strikes the middle ring of the cruel heart, you win the cutest stuffed bunny!"

"Speaking of bunnies, I'd better check on the pet show," said Rapunzel.

"I should start warming up for masketball," said Cinda.

Red whipped her cape open and flung out her arms in a dramatic way. "And I, Red Robin Hood, need to rehearse so that I may foil that scoundrel of a sheriff during my performance tonight in a proper fashion." She bounded off for the amphitheater with exaggerated leaps that made her friends giggle.

The afternoon passed quickly as Rapunzel helped out the little kids, and grown-ups, too, who'd come from all over the realm to bring animals for the pet show. In the end, she gave out the prize ribbons she'd made to everyone who entered, so all would go home with smiles on their faces. Mordred showed up just in time for the judging and was awarded a ribbon for Best Cat with a White Star. He practically grinned!

For a moment, he posed with his ribbon like the most refined, regal cat in all of Grimmlandia. Then he leaped into a bed of straw Rapunzel had spread on the ground and ran around and around in circles. Two other cats joined in and a fray began with them rolling in the hay. Looking gleeful and somewhat like a straw-quilled porcupine, her cat then dashed off across the festival grounds. To get into more mischief, no doubt, Rapunzel thought fondly.

After the pet show, she headed for the food area. Mistress Hagscorch, Ms. Queenharts, and Ms. Jabberwocky had all decorated their gazebos with themes related to the snacks they'd created. Based on her Rampion Championship idea, Hagscorch had turned her gazebo into a cute ship with flags flying from the spire on its roof, and sails around the sides. Although Rapunzel hadn't spoken to her, she was sure the cook must've found the rampion left in her icebox. Because she would've kept bugging Rapunzel about it if she hadn't!

Ms. Queenharts's gazebo was decorated to look like a small castle with gleaming suits of armor standing around to guard it. Each "knight" wore a red paper heart on its chest with the word *Tarts* written upon it in white chalk.

Not to be outdone, Ms. Jabberwocky, a dragon-lady who actually breathed fire, had painted canvas panels with various wild dragons and hung them around her snack gazebo.

"Wow! Hagscorch has gone all out!" said Red. She and the other actors had come by the food gazebos after rehearsal at the island amphitheater to eat before their play began at sunset. "She made Huffing Puffs, Doomdogs and Gloomburgers, Tickle Pickles, and Gargoyle Pops. And watch this." Red held up an I Scream Cone, and when she bit into it, it let out a bloodcurdling scream!

"That big Rampion Championship she made is so cute," added Snow. "And huge. I like that she made it ship-shaped, too. She won't let anyone try it yet, though. Said she's saving it for tomorrow night as a prize for the overall champion of the festival. Get it? It's a *ship* for *champions*. I think she's sure to win the competition for best snacks."

Wolfgang came over, munching on something. "I don't know about that. Ms. Queenharts's tarts are pretty awesome," he said.

"Did someone call me?" It was Prince Awesome, grinning. He was eating a tart, too, and gave Cinda a bite.

"Mmm," she said approvingly.

"Ms. Jabberwocky's barbecue peppers are pretty cool — I mean hot!" said Basil. "They actually make flames come out of your mouth for a few seconds after you eat them. Behold." He took a bite of a pepper. Then he breathed outward, saying, "Ooh! *Hhhot* stuff." Everyone jumped back as sizzling flames shot from his lips. Then they all laughed hysterically.

Ms. Jabberwocky's food might be flaming, but the other two cooks themselves were steaming, Rapunzel noted. As in steaming mad. They'd begun arguing. She turned her attention from her friends and listened to the cooks to discover what the problem was.

"You stole my tarts idea," Hagscorch was saying. "But I'll still win the Best Snack Award!"

"Ha! We'll just see about that! And by the way, you stole from me first," Queenharts replied.

Mistress Hagscorch rolled her eyes. "I had nothing to do with that knave stealing your tart that summer's day. If I had stolen your recipe, my tarts would taste like yours, but mine are far superior."

"What makes you two think you'll win anyway?" demanded Ms. Jabberwocky, popping a barbecue pepper in

116

her mouth. "My pppeppers are pppretty pppopppular." Each time she spoke a *p*, flames shot from her green snout.

Oh, hagsnaggle! thought Rapunzel. Would an all-out war break out among these cooks when the Best Snack Award was announced? It seemed obvious that the two who didn't win would be annoyed, and that could ruin the festival. Their arguing might not end here, either. They might very well keep it up at the Academy next week. Although Red was in charge of the food and this was technically her problem, this was the first break she'd had all day from preparations for her play. Not wanting to bother her right now, Rapunzel took charge.

"Maybe there could be three snack awards instead of one," she suggested brightly. "Best tart. Most unusual ship snack. Most fiery snack. What do you say? Three awards, and you guys stop arguing. Is it a deal?"

"Forget it," said Hagscorch, shaking her head.

"No way," said Queenharts, crossing her arms. "It's obvious who'd win those from the get-go."

"Let everyone at the festival vote on the snacks for one award as planned. And may the best cook win," said Ms. Jabberwocky.

"That will be me," said Queenharts.

"We'll see about that," said Hagscorch.

"Hhha!" huffed Jabberwocky, letting out another blast of flames.

Apparently, I learned nothing in Mr. Dickory's class, thought Rapunzel in dismay. She still super stunk at bargaining!

Just then, Snow called out to her. "Let's grab a few more snacks and go watch some of the games until it's time for Red's play."

Rapunzel nodded, and minutes later, she, Snow, and Red were wandering through the various sports and games. First, they watched Cinda's masketball game. She was play-ing on the team opposite Awesome's. Since the two of them were evenly matched stars, the scores were close all game long. It was hard to tell who was who since everyone wore magical masks, but when one of the shortest players dunked the ball in the final moments to win, the three Grimm girls whooped and waved excitedly in the stands. Since most of the players were tall boys, they just knew the scoring player had to be Cinda!

Afterward, Cinda joined them in exploring the festi-val. Munching Gloomburgers and Huffing Puffs, Rapunzel relaxed, thinking how nice it was just hanging out with her besties and forgetting about her troubles for a while. It was almost sunset when the four Grimm girl friends came upon Basil and Prince Prince, who were competing in the siege games on the lawn against Foulsmell and Awesome.

As Rapunzel stood cheering wildly for Basil, she felt a tap on her shoulder. She turned to find Prince Perfect standing there. He looked so cute in his dark blue tunic, she thought as he bowed to her. "Would you do me the honor of accompanying me to the Festival Ball tonight?" he asked.

Stunned speechless, she nodded. At her reply, Perfect grinned and bowed again, then walked away. She turned back toward her friends, her eyes wide.

"Did he just ask you to —" Snow began.

"Go with him —" Red added.

"To the ball?" Cinda finished.

Rapunzel nodded, feeling dazed and happy.

"Awesome," said Cinda. "Oh, and I'm going with Awesome, too," she added with a giggle.

"And Wolfgang asked me," said Red.

"And I'll be with Prince Prince," finished Snow.

"It's going to be sooo fun!" said Rapunzel. The four Grimm girls started jumping around in excitement.

Just then, another round of contestants was announced in the siege games on the lawn. Snow and Cinda were up next. Red wished them good luck, then departed for rehearsals again. Rapunzel gave her a quick encouraging hug, and stayed behind to watch the other two girls compete.

"Perfect. Just perfect. Do you Grimm girls have to take all the cute boys at GA for yourselves?" complained a voice. Rapunzel looked over to see Mary Mary Quite Contrary standing beside her, arms folded. The girl turned to go, mumbling, "That old lady in the forest was a big fat liar."

119

"What?" asked Rapunzel in surprise. But the girl had already stomped off.

Rapunzel ran after her. "Wait. What did you say? What old lady?"

"The one in Neverwood Forest that you were talking to Thursday," Mary Mary told her grumpily.

"You saw me?" Rapunzel squeaked in surprise. Suddenly, she recalled the extra boat that had been onshore when she and Snow rowed away from the woods. "You followed me, didn't you? Why?"

Mary Mary shrugged. "To see why you were acting so sneaky. I mean, who goes off to Neverwood alone? I thought maybe you were meeting . . ." Her eyes flicked to Perfect, who was now over with Basil and the other boys. She sighed and stomped off again.

Rapunzel fell into step beside her. "And the old lady?"

"She gave me the comb. That one I loaned you in Threads," Mary Mary admitted. "Asked me to get you to use it. She said it would fix your hair wiggles, so I figured, why not?"

"Oh, no!" said Rapunzel, hearing that dreaded word. Would her hair behave itself?

Thinking she was mad now, Mary Mary darted her a look. "The only reason I'm telling you this is so you know I tried. I do feel kind of guilty about that tongue twister accident. But it looks like your hair is still wiggly, so I guess she lied about fixing that, too."

"Too?" Rapunzel echoed. Her braid was indeed acting bonkerdoodles again thanks to Mary Mary's use of the word *wiggle*. She wrapped it around her waist and held it there with one hand. Just then, a cheer went up from the crowd around the siege competition. The boys were now catapulting pumpkins they'd decorated earlier, which exploded on impact. She and Rapunzel looked over in time to see Prince Perfect launch his.

Mary Mary sighed admiringly. "He's just so . . . *perfect*. The old lady told me he'd ask me to the ball, but —"

Rapunzel frowned. So that was it. The deal. She'd guessed from the start that the "old lady" must be the witch. And she only ever made deals that benefited herself. She must've promised Mary Mary that she'd win Perfect's favor in exchange for giving Rapunzel the comb. But why?

"Where's the comb now?" she asked the girl. She started braiding her hair again, trying to calm it down.

Mary Mary snapped her fingers. "*Poof*! It vamoosed into thin air right after I left Threads class yesterday. Now stop following me."

Mary Mary stomped off again. Rapunzel watched her go, not sure what to do. Poor Mary Mary, her heart broken by that dumb witch. Still, even if Perfect hadn't asked

Rapunzel to the ball, she wouldn't have been able to make him ask Mary Mary. Or anyone else, for that matter.

Noticing that one of her potted bouquets had gotten knocked over, Mary Mary stopped and picked it up. With a mere touch of her fingers, the flowers magically mended themselves, perking up again. How nice. That kind of magic was the good kind and made Rapunzel feel happy. It was quite different from the witch's brand of magic. The evil kind the witch hoped to teach Rapunzel.

Speaking of magic, Rapunzel suddenly remembered how much she'd longed for that comb as soon as she'd seen it. It must have been bespelled by the witch! Luckily, whatever the witch's intent in getting Rapunzel to use it, her comb hadn't succeeded. At least Rapunzel hoped not.

Hearing someone shout her name, she turned to see Basil.

"Rapunzel, wait up!" he called as he loped over. When he reached her, he just stood there acting all nervous. He appeared to be tongue-tied and his hands were fidgeting at his sides. Which was weird. Basil was usually so confident and easygoing — traits she admired in him.

"What's up?" she asked him.

"I was wondering . . ." His words petered out and he shifted from one booted foot to the other. His hair flopped cutely over his forehead and she watched him push it back.

Finally, he tried again. "I was wondering . . . would you like to go to the Festival Ball. With me?"

She stared at him in surprise. Then she lightly punched his shoulder and laughed off his offer, figuring he was just being nice. "You don't have to do that. Perfect asked me. But save me a dance, okay?"

"Perfect?" Basil's eyes widened for a moment. Then he started backing away. "Oh. Yeah. Sure. Well, it looks like that *Red Robin Hood* play's getting ready to start. I told Wolfgang I'd help with, um, some stage stuff. See you." He jogged off. He'd sounded really disappointed! But why would he be? They were just buddies . . . weren't they?

It was almost dark now, and she hadn't been able to see his expression that well. Had she only imagined his hurt feelings? *Oh, bopnoddle!* she thought. Why did boys have to be so confusing?

Rapunzel started to go after Basil, then paused when she heard a faint cry. It sounded kind of familiar. She cocked her ear to better hear it, but the sound had faded away.

By now, most people had taken seats in the amphitheater, since Red and Wolfgang and the rest of the cast would begin performing in a few minutes. From a distance, she spotted Cinda and Snow in the audience and headed their way, still mulling over what Mary Mary had said about the comb. *Why had the witch made that deal with her?* she wondered.

Over at the theater, the red velvet curtains swept open for Act One of *Red Robin Hood*. The play was the last event of today's festival. But tomorrow, Sunday, the fun would all begin again, and end in the Festival Ball Sunday night. The one she was going to with her crush! Rapunzel lifted the hem of her gown slightly and hurried toward the theater. She wanted to take a seat before Red made her entrance.

Then she stopped, hearing that weird cry again. It was Mordred! *Howling.* It sounded like he was in trouble!

Swinging around, Rapunzel turned and ran toward the sound, following as it led her toward the tower. The moon was bright enough to light her way, and there were candles flickering in decorative stone stands here and there around the festival grounds. Just as she rounded the trees, the howling stopped. And there stood the witch! She was alone at the base of the tower, her eyes glittering.

"Where's my cat?" Rapunzel demanded in a panicked voice. When the witch didn't reply, Rapunzel turned on her heel to continue looking for Mordred elsewhere.

"I have your magic charm," said the witch. Rapunzel looked over one shoulder and watched the witch reach into her black bag. She pulled out the onyx comb. The fanciful carved one Mary Mary had loaned her in Threads class.

Rapunzel shook her head. "That's not mine."

The witch stepped closer. "It is. Your parents wanted you to havc it."

Rapunzel gasped. "No way. My parents were poor. They couldn't afford such a fine comb. Besides, they bargained me away to you for a bit of rampion. I obviously wasn't that important to them."

The witch's brows rose. "It's true that they didn't have much money. But your father found a piece of onyx and made this comb for you based on your mother's design. It's your charm, all right. Cross my heart."

The witch hadn't disagreed when Rapunzel said she wasn't that important to her parents, Rapunzel noticed. So maybe she agreed that they hadn't really loved her. But then why had they bothered to make her something so valuable and pretty?

The witch took another step forward and held out the comb. However, when Rapunzel reached for it, she quickly snatched it back. With an air of satisfaction, she said, "I'll give it to you on one condition. That you use it now to comb out your hair."

Rapunzel's eyes gleamed as she stared at the comb. If it really was her charm — one that her parents had made for her — then she wanted it desperately. But she held back.

"Why should I believe you?" she asked the witch. "You lied to Mary Mary. Besides, charms only do what the person they belong to tells them to do, and that comb is obeying you."

Meowww! It was Mordred howling again. She could tell that the witch heard him, too. And from the cruel smile on her face, Rapunzel guessed she had something to do with whatever trouble her cat was so obviously in.

Without waiting for a reply, Rapunzel ran around to the other side of the tower. Mordred howled again, and this time she could tell that he was somewhere above her. She tilted her head back to gaze at the tower's single high window. There he sat on the window ledge. The witch must have magicked him up there somehow, because there was no way he could've gotten to the top of the tower by himself!

Rapunzel looked around desperately for some way to reach him. Apparently, no one had succeeded in getting one of the ropes up to the window. They all still lay coiled on the ground.

"It's okay, Mordred," she said soothingly. "I'll figure out a way to get you down." Maybe she could throw the rope herself, climb it, and rescue him. Not likely, but it was her only hope. She ran toward the tower, reaching for one of the coils. As her fingers touched the rope, there was a loud grinding noise.

And suddenly the tower disappeared, taking Mordred with it!

9

Tower Power

The witch had disappeared, too, and Rapunzel knew of only one place to look for her and the tower. And most of all, Mordred! She just hoped her cat would be safe till she could rescue him. She ran down to the dock and leaped into one of the swan boats. Hearing footsteps, she turned and saw that Snow and Cinda had followed her. They must have seen her leaving the amphitheater.

"Red's onstage. You're missing out on a grimmtabulous performance," Cinda told her.

"Yeah. Where are you going?" asked Snow.

"Please don't ask," Rapunzel replied. On an impulse, she jumped from the boat to hug them both. If she went into Neverwood Forest and met up with the witch, who knew what might happen? This might be good-bye forever!

"Is this about that witch?" Snow guessed. "I mean the one who raised her," she added to Cinda, who was looking puzzled.

Rapunzel was too upset to hold back what was happening

any longer. "Yes! I think she might have magicked that Tower of Doom from the festival back to Neverwood. With Mordred inside!"

She climbed back into the swan boat again and picked up a paddle.

"You're not going into that forest alone to find him!" said Snow. She and Cinda jumped into the boat before Rapunzel could stop them.

"But it could be very, very dangerous," Rapunzel protested.

Cinda sent her a supportive smile. "Hello? You sound like Mr. Hump-Dumpty!"

"If you're going, we're going," Snow added firmly. The two girls picked up paddles. And together they shoved off. The Once Upon River looked almost black at night, but the full moon led them toward Neverwood's shore. On the boat trip over, Rapunzel filled them in on the details of what had happened with the witch, including the comb.

Soon they were inside the forest, scurrying down a path. Tree roots crawled near their feet and tried to trip them as they ran. Oddly, torches hung in the trees, their flames swaying in the breeze. *Is the witch lighting our way?* Rapunzel wondered. In no time at all, they reached the clearing.

"There!" shouted Snow. Sure enough, the tower loomed before them.

Meooowww! Mordred howled from its window. Again Rapunzel wondered how the witch had achieved magic strong enough to transport him and the tower here.

"Don't be scared. I'm here, Mordred," she called softly as the three Grimm girls stepped into the rampion patch. The green stalks with their pretty pale purple bellflowers rustled around their skirts.

Instantly, the witch appeared before them. Ignoring Snow and Cinda completely, she said to Rapunzel, "He'll make a fine companion, once I train him to do my bidding." She waved a hand toward the tower and the cat stopped howling.

"No! Let him go!" Rapunzel begged. Then she winced, remembering that begging was something Mr. Dickory had specifically told students not to do when making a bargain. And wasn't that what this was — a deal in the making? She wanted her cat back safe and sound, and the witch wanted something else. But just exactly what, she wasn't quite sure.

The witch held the comb out again. "The cat will be set free if you do as I ask. All you have to do is comb your hair."

Comb her hair? That was the deal? If so, it was sure to be a *bad* one for Rapunzel. She just wished she knew what the witch was up to.

"Don't do it," Cinda whispered from behind her.

Mr. Dickory had told them, "Don't be afraid to leave a bad deal." But if Rapunzel tried that, would the witch really call her back and suggest something better? She couldn't take the chance. Not with Mordred at risk. So what choice did she have?

"Her cat's up there. She has to save him!" Snow whispered to Cinda.

The two girls continued whispering, but Rapunzel hardly heard them. She was staring at the comb, mesmerized. Had her father really made it? she wondered. The more she looked at the beautiful comb, the more she wanted it. Was it enchanted? It must be because she'd fallen under its spell! As the seconds passed, the witch's bargain didn't seem so horrible anymore. All at once, Rapunzel reached out for the comb. She grabbed it and began running it through her long glossy black hair.

The witch smiled a ghastly smile. Worried now, Rapunzel stopped combing. "Did you put a spell on this thing?"

"Of course," cackled the witch. "A two-parter. After you combed your hair with it in class, it caused your hair to do my bidding in the Grimmstone Library. But the spell wasn't complete until you combed your hair a second time just now."

"What's she talking about?" she heard Cinda whisper behind her.

"No clue," Snow replied.

They hadn't learned multipart spells in Bespellings class yet, but Rapunzel knew they were far more powerful than single spells. Having no idea what the witch had actually done, she dropped the precious comb into her bag.

But the witch didn't seem to care. She was studying the treetops. "Your parents and I made a bargain. A bargain in which they gave you — and all your belongings — to me. Including that comb. However, it has now served its purpose. You can keep it."

"Let Mordred go," Rapunzel demanded. "And we'll be on our way."

"In a moment. When I have what I want."

"What *do* you want?"

The witch eyed her. Then she drew in a sharp breath and pointed a bony finger into the distant sky. "Those!"

The three Grimm girls gasped as artifacts slowly began floating toward them through the shadowy trees. They drifted one by one into the clearing, all coming from the direction of the Academy. First came a queen chess piece gleaming white in the darkness. It was followed by a toy rabbit and cockle shells. The witch held her bag open and the objects dropped inside, one after the other.

"*Q, R, S.* They're in alphabetical order," Rapunzel murmured. And they looked familiar. She glanced back at her friends. "My w-i-g-g-l-y hair touched each of those things in the library yesterday. It must've been *choosing* them."

"Choosing them for me. And for a certain society I

belong to!" The witch let out a huge cackle that echoed throughout the forest.

Cinda gasped. "She's helping the E.V.I.L. Society!"

She and Snow stepped toward the witch as if hoping to somehow stop her. Immediately, the rampion stalks rustled. Vines slithered lower, curling like snakes around their feet and ankles. "I can't move!" said Snow.

"Me neither," said Cinda. "We're trapped!"

Rapunzel felt the vines ensnare her ankles as well. She looked back at the others. "Moving will only make it worse," she warned them in a whisper. "Stay still for now." As a girl, she'd watched from her high window many times as the witch had used this trick to trap passing strangers and make deals that cheated them out of riches or information.

"You're right, little Grimm girls, I'm collecting artifacts for E.V.I.L.!" the witch crowed as the objects continued to fall into her bag. Next came a *T* and a *U* — a teacup, then an umbrella. The bag magically expanded as it filled. "They're my ticket to fame."

"Fame?" Rapunzel's brows rose in confusion.

The witch shot her an irritated glance. "What's my name?" All three girls stared at her blankly.

"You don't have a name," Rapunzel replied after a few seconds of silence. "You're simply called the witch in my fairy tale."

At her words, the witch's sour expression turned angry. "Exactly! *The Witch.* But you girls do have actual names, don't you? Wilhelm and Jacob Grimm saw to that when they wrote your tales. Evil characters always get the short end of the stick, yet we're the most important characters in any story, if you ask me. Well, E.V.I.L.'s leader has figured out how to fix all that so it's fair. By stealing artifacts!" She darted over to stand in a new spot and held her bag wider. A violin playing a dreamy melody dropped into it.

"But how will stealing artifacts get you a name in the great books of Grimm?" asked Snow.

"Simple, dear girl." The witch rushed over to catch two more artifacts that drifted in from the forest. A pocket watch and a ball of yellow yarn, Rapunzel noted in alarm. Only a *Z* artifact was left to reach the end of the alphabet!

"Soon the wall will break open and our leader will step through it," the witch went on. "He'll overtake the Grimmstone Library and rewrite the books of Grimm. And the nursery rhymes and folktales, too, while he's at it. Readers everywhere will be easily convinced that the evil characters — who will all be given names — are the ones to admire in the tales. Not the goody-two-shoes characters like you."

"No way!" argued Cinda.

"Get used to it!" ranted the witch. "Soon we evil characters will be the stars, not the likes of you." She paused. "For example," she said to Rapunzel, "I plan to change the name of *our* fairy tale."

Rapunzel's jaw dropped. "No, you wouldn't . . . you couldn't . . ."

"Yes! And I'm going to call myself Wonderful Witch Twitch," the witch said proudly. "That's the name I've chosen for myself in the new improved tale the Society will write. However, you'll only be mentioned as the girl with long hair. The tale known as *Rapunzel* will change forevermore to a new title, *The Wonderful Witch Twitch and the Rotten Long-Haired Girl.* How will you like that? Not much, I bet!" The witch threw back her head and let out another horrible cackling laugh that sent chills up Rapunzel's spine.

The three girls stared at one another in horror. "If you change our tales, it could lead to an epic Grimmlandian disaster you didn't anticipate and won't at all like," Rapunzel warned.

Snow nodded. "Even a little change could have a ripple effect. Like dominoes falling one after another, the stories will come apart when their morals don't make sense anymore."

"Which would be dastardly for good and evil characters alike," added Cinda. "Dire, in fact!"

Now they all three sounded as worried as Mr. Hump-Dumpty. But with good reason. The witch's plan was major bad news.

"So be it," hissed the witch, not seeming to care. Just then, a small ceramic zebra dropped into her bag. Kicking up her heels with joy, she snatched the bag closed. Then she eyed Rapunzel. "We have twenty-six artifacts now. One for every letter in the alphabet. Letters make words. Words make stories. And stories can be changed with strong enough magic — Grimm family magic. Soon the wall around Grimmlandia will open. And at last, our leader will take his rightful place within the tales."

Huh? thought Rapunzel. What did that mean?

The witch didn't linger to be questioned. She rubbed a gold ring she wore on her left hand. Rapunzel couldn't recall her ever wearing such a ring when she'd lived in the tower. But for some reason, it looked familiar.

Before she could get a better look at it, the witch disappeared in a cloud of black smoke, taking the tower and artifacts with her. Only she left the cat behind, standing in the flattened area in the middle of the rampion patch where the tower had once stood.

Meowww!

"Mordred!" Once the witch departed, the vines fell away from the girls' ankles, and Rapunzel scurried over to him. Luckily, he was unharmed. Scooping him up and holding him close, she followed her friends as they dashed out of the rampion patch, heading for shore again. The torches had died out, and only the moonlight filtering through the trees allowed them to find their way back to the swan boats.

Once there, Rapunzel sat cuddling Mordred while Snow and Cinda paddled toward the Academy. She murmured sweet words to him as they crossed the river. Over at Heart Island, fireworks began, lighting up the night sky. That meant the play had ended and the festival was closing for the day.

Upon their return to the Academy, Mordred leaped away and dashed ahead to Rapunzel's room, none the worse for his adventure. The girls found Red and they all gathered in the dungeon, sitting on Rapunzel's bed.

"Lucky for you guys, there will be another performance of our play in the school auditorium in a few days," Red informed them right off the bat.

"Oh, good! I feel so bad we missed seeing it!" Cinda replied, her blue eyes wide with distress.

"Me, too!" said Snow. "It's just awful. Not your *play*. I'm sure it was great. I just meant that it's too bad we —"

"I understood what you meant," Red said, grinning a little at Snow's consternation.

"We wouldn't have missed it for anything. Except we were busy trying to foil a witch's evil plot," Rapunzel added.

"What?" said Red, instantly alarmed. Quickly, the other girls explained all that had happened since they'd last seen her. "If the tales get changed so that evil wins, well, that's just wrong!" Red pronounced, sounding worried.

"Yeah. Readers will start to believe that good charac-ters like us acted badly and that evil is actually good!" said Cinda. "Which is what the witch hopes!"

"Ooh! I almost forgot." Red pulled the mapestry out of her basket. "I checked this thing right after the play. And look! The *X* moved from the island over to Neverwood Forest!"

The girls crowded around eagerly as she unrolled the mapestry. However, to Red's surprise, the *X* was right there where it had always been — on Heart Island. "Weird. I thought for sure — but I guess I was wrong."

"Or maybe the *X* moved because we did? Or because Mordred did. Or the tower. Or the swan boat we took over there," mused Rapunzel. "But that would have to mean that one of us has the treasure, or that . . ." She stopped talking, confused.

"Or any of a dozen possibilities," Snow put in. The four Grimm girls talked and talked, but by bedtime, they still hadn't figured out why the X might have temporarily moved or what to do about the witch and the Society's evil plot. Hoping the answers might lie in the library, they decided to meet there the next morning.

Hours later, in the middle of the night, Rapunzel sud-denly awoke and sat up in bed. The four cats on her comforter stirred, blinking at her. Over on the windowsill, Mordred lifted his head. Quickly, she counted on her fingers. Twenty-six. Twenty-six artifacts had been collected by E.V.I.L. There were twenty-six letters in the alphabet. But E.V.I.L. had collected *two P* artifacts — Jack and Jill's pail and Peter Peter's pumpkin. Which meant that a missing letter and its corresponding artifact had yet to fall into their grasp!

Unable to sleep, she hopped out of bed and began to pace, thinking hard. As she walked, she combed her hair with her new charm. *What powers does it possess?* she wondered.

"I hope I find out before too long," she murmured. Long. *Long.* The word seemed to hum in the air around her. Suddenly, the teeth of the comb started growing longer. And longer. She dropped it, leaping back, and watched it grow as tall as she was. What had just happened? Did the comb think she had commanded it?

"Short," she whispered uncertainly.

Instantly, the comb's teeth shortened to normal length again. She picked up the comb from the floor and gazed at it in wonder. "That was grimmazing!" she told it. "I wonder what else you can do?"

But it seemed she was not destined to find out. For, suddenly, the comb disappeared from her hand. *Poof!* That lying witch! She must have used her magic to steal it back again.

10

The Plan

$\mathcal{S}$unday morning, while everyone else headed to Heart Island for the second day of the festival, Red, Cinda, Snow, and Rapunzel met in the Grimm brothers' room in the library.

The objects there seemed unusually restless. Small wind-up toys zoomed across the floor, knocking into each other like bumper cars. A mechanical toy monkey sat alone in a corner, frantically clapping its cymbals together. And over on the shelf of musical instruments, the flute and harmonica were playing an eerie, discordant duet. At the same time, the great books of Grimm were pulling themselves out of the shelves, flipping upside down, and then sliding back in again, over and over.

Gazing around at the strange scene, Rapunzel announced to her friends, "I realized something important last night. The witch found twenty-six artifacts. But two of them started with *P*. And when Cinda and I were in here yesterday, a hand reached out of the coat of arms. And a voice asked for the *X*. It wanted the *X* artifact that E.V.I.L. is missing! I'm pretty sure it's the —"

"Xylophone?" Cinda guessed, pointing toward the shelf of musical instruments where it sat.

The other three Grimm girls turned just in time to see its two mallets rise in the air. Then they skimmed up and down the xylophone's bars, creating a cascade of ascending and descending notes.

"I think so. On Friday, my hair put a spell on each artifact the witch wanted, simply by touching it," Rapunzel explained. "But because we brought the xylophone in here instead of leaving it on the main library shelves, the room's extra protections must have kept it from being stolen. Even the geese helpers in the library won't come inside this room."

"I get it. So you don't think any E.V.I.L. members will come in here either?" asked Red.

"Maybe not," said Rapunzel.

Snow set the Handbook she'd brought with her on top of the Grimm brothers' big desk. "I bet you're right. My stepmom once told me this room gives her the creeps. She refuses to get anywhere near it."

"Which means that this is probably the safest place in all of Grimmlandia," said Rapunzel. "A place where evil can't go. We've seen the leader try to enter this room through the coat of arms. But he couldn't, remember?"

"What do you think the witch will do when she realizes the X artifact is missing?" asked Cinda.

"If we can think of something to stop her and E.V.I.L., maybe we won't have to find out," said Red. Suddenly, her attention was caught by something on the opposite wall. Slowly, she asked, "Hey, what did that ring you said the witch was wearing look like?"

"It was gold with jewels and had a letter engraved in its center," Snow told her.

"Like those?" Red pointed at the seven gold-framed portraits hanging in the center of the wall opposite the desk.

The girls turned to study them. All the faces looked similar, as if they were related to each other. And on the hand of each person pictured was a matching gold ring!

"Yes! The ring the witch was wearing looked exactly the same," said Rapunzel. "I thought it seemed familiar. Must've been because I'd seen it in these paintings."

"So these portraits . . . are they all Grimms?" asked Cinda.

Snow opened her Handbook to History class and found a chapter titled "The Grimm Family." She pressed on a word, causing a bubble to rise and hover a foot above the page. There were seven faces in the bubble, each one labeled with a name. The girls compared them, matching the names and faces in the bubble to the portraits on the wall.

"That's Jacob and Wilhelm on top, of course," said Red. Everyone in Grimmlandia knew what they looked like. There were likenesses of them carved on buildings and fountains in every village, and portraits of them hung in museums throughout the realm. "And we know that's their sister, Charlotte the Enchantress, from when she was a lot younger than she is now."

"The others are Friedrich, Carl, and Ferdinand," Snow told them. "So the one under that drape must be . . ."

As she spoke, Red went over and lifted the drape covering the central painting. Cinda, Rapunzel, and Snow gasped at the sight of the face she revealed. "Eek! It's *him*!" yelled Cinda and Snow at the same time.

"Who?" asked Red.

"The nose-eyeball guy I saw in here on my first day at the Academy," Cinda explained.

"And I saw him on my stepmom's door that time," Snow confirmed.

"He's the only one not wearing a ring," noted Rapunzel, pointing to his hand.

"Could the witch have his?" Cinda wondered.

As they were talking, Snow began thumbing through her Handbook again. "It says here that one Grimm brother disappeared from Grimmlandia years ago. His name was Ludwig."

"Ludwig," whispered a woman's voice at the same time. At the sound of the disembodied voice, the girls shrieked in alarm and looked wildly around the room.

"Who said that?" Rapunzel whispered.

Red pushed aside a few papers and discovered a crystal ball sitting on the desktop. "It's Grandmother Enchantress!" She pointed to the ancient-looking face of a woman that gazed at them from within the ball.

The girls crowded around the desk. "How did her crystal ball wind up in here?" asked Cinda.

"Shh! She's trying to tell us something," said Snow as a pink sparkly mist began to spin around the face inside the ball.

"I moved . . . crystal . . . here. . . . It's . . . only safe place . . . now . . . evil . . . growing stronger," rasped the Enchantress. Her voice was weak and faded in and out, making it hard to understand her. "A meeting . . . E.V.I.L. Society . . . today . . . Heart Island."

"When exactly?" asked Cinda. But the sparkly mist had faded away from the crystal ball, and the Enchantress said no more.

"I'm confused," Snow said. "How could Ludwig be the leader of the Society? The Grimm brothers are all long dead, aren't they? I thought only Charlotte . . . that is, Grandmother Enchantress, was still alive."

"Maybe they're like the library," suggested Rapunzel. She quoted Ms. Goose: "Magical, movable, timeless."

"Or maybe they just all disappeared into the Dark Nothingterror," Cinda said in a small voice. There was a brief silence as everyone digested that horrible thought. The Nothingterror was the area beyond the wall that surrounded Grimmlandia, and was a terrible place said to be filled with beasts and dastardlies.

"Listen to this," said Snow, consulting her Handbook again. "Ludwig didn't just disappear. He was *banished* to the other side of the wall. This says he was a talented artist, but not as famous as Jacob and Wilhelm. So he grew resentful and jealous of his brothers' fame. And he harbored a prejudice against fairy-tale characters, especially the 'good' ones. He was basically the black sheep of the Grimm family!"

"We have to find out what's going on in that E.V.I.L. meeting on the island today. But the Society isn't going to be happy with us if they catch us spying. We'd better take something to bargain with just in case," said Red.

"We know what they'll want," said Cinda, glancing toward the xylophone.

They all followed her gaze. "No! We can't give it to them. Can we?" asked Snow.

"Hmm. Maybe we can," said Rapunzel. Quickly, she told them what she was thinking, and they worked out a plan.

A few minutes later, the girls scurried out of the room to pick up the ball gowns and slippers they would wear to the ball later that night. While in the library's *S* section for their slippers, Rapunzel brought everyone to a halt to take a look at the *Spells to Foil Fairy-Tale Crooks* book she'd discovered on Friday.

"Eew," said Cinda, scrunching her nose at the chapter titles in the table of contents. "I'm not sure I could hook or cook anyone, no matter how evil they were. Not even a witch or a troll."

"Me, neither," said Rapunzel. "But could we try this?" She showed them another chapter in the book and they all crowded around to skim it together. Excitement filled everyone's eyes as she snapped the book shut, because what she'd read just might help them stop the witch! She put the book away and they picked up their slippers.

In the *G* section, Snow, Cinda, and Red got their gowns and Rapunzel's, too, while she detoured to one of the *G* bookshelves. There, she signed the tag that allowed her to check out a book of Grimm Fairy Tales. When the girls met up again, Rapunzel handed Red the book to slip into her basket. One last stop by Snow's trunker so she could drop off her Handbook and grab her magic charm tiara, then the four girls were finally off to Heart Island, their arms full of satin, silk, and slippers.

On the way out of the Academy, they passed Mary Mary

in the Bouquet Garden. "Isn't this day bee-yoo-teeful?" she enthused, beaming at them. She was holding a pair of pruning shears as she snipped off her flowers' spent blossoms.

The girls stared at her in stunned surprise, nodding. The weather was indeed perfect for the final day of the festival. The sky was a beautiful blue with some small puffy white clouds. But for Mary Mary to act so upbeat was unusual, to say the least.

"Well, farewell for now. I'll see you on the island once I finish here. And have a happily ever day!" she told them, her smile growing even wider.

"Why is she so happy?" Snow whispered to the other three BFFs as they headed for the swan boats.

"I think it's because her cockleshells are missing from the library now," whispered Rapunzel. "Remember the rumor? Not only are they her charm as well as an artifact, they're also what makes her contrary, like in her nursery rhyme."

"I didn't think a charm could also be an artifact," said Snow.

"Leave it to her to have one that is *contrary* to the rules!" joked Cinda.

"Well, I just hope we recover those shells," said Red. "It's weird seeing her act so cheery. Can you imagine having that go on forever, this year and the next and on and on?"

The others giggled. All except Rapunzel. She was thinking that if that happened, she wouldn't be here to witness it.

She didn't say a word until they were seated in one of the swan boats. Then she blurted out what was on her mind. "Even if we save the Academy before Monday, I won't be going to school here next year."

Her friends all stared at her in surprise. "What do you mean? Why not?" Red demanded.

"It's because of a deal I made with the witch when I was six," Rapunzel admitted in a rush. She glanced at Snow, who already knew the story, of course, and Snow nodded encouragement for her to go on.

"She wouldn't let me start first grade at GA unless I promised in exchange that when I turned thirteen, I'd go back to work for her again," Rapunzel told Red and Cinda. "And let her teach me the Dark Arts."

"It's awful, isn't it?" Snow said. "Thirteen can be such an unlucky number!" Snow believed in luck, both good and bad.

"Well, we can't let it happen," Red fumed.

"You know what?" Cinda told Rapunzel defiantly as they all began paddling. "I bet someone powerful like Principal R or the Grimm brothers or the Enchantress told that witch to send you to GA, but then she pretended it was her idea. Which would mean the deal she made with you wasn't fair!"

"Besides, you were only six," added Red. "You can't be held to a bargain you made when you were that little."

"You have to stay at GA," Cinda said softly from beside her. She gave Rapunzel a hug. "We'll miss you too much if you go." Red and Snow leaned forward from their seats and joined in, wrapping their arms about Rapunzel and Cinda.

Their support touched Rapunzel's heart and she felt tears burn in her eyes. "Thanks, you guys. I want to stay. I'd miss you, too," she said when they finally broke apart.

To her friends' credit, none of them had acted the least bit appalled when she'd mentioned that she might have to learn the Dark Arts. Maybe they trusted that whatever the witch taught her, she would never use it for evil. She brushed away her tears and began to paddle again as new determination filled her. She would beat the witch at her own evil game. She had to. They all had to. The consequences would be too devastating if they didn't. For her personally, and for the whole Academy as well!

11

E.V.I.L.

"Look! It's back!" said Cinda.

When they pulled up to Heart Island in the swan boat, Rapunzel, Red, Cinda, and Snow spotted the tower right away. Before going to investigate, they took their gowns and slippers over to the big white tent that had been set up on the far shore. It overlooked the river and the Academy and was where the Festival Ball would take place that night. They would return here to don their gowns later that afternoon in the girls' side of the changing rooms before the ball.

If there is a ball, Rapunzel thought, her confidence wavering. Would Grimm Academy triumph by the end of the day? Or would E.V.I.L. win?

After looking around to be sure no one was watching her, Snow pressed the largest sparkly turquoise jewel on the front of the cute tiara she wore. Instantly, she went invisible. "You guys take care of all the festival stuff, okay? I'm off to spy on my stepmom to see if I can find out when that meeting is," she told the others. "Wish me luck!"

"We do!" Cinda assured her.

Rapunzel left soon after on a very important errand of her own. There was something she needed to find — fast. The dark tower peeking from the trees seemed to mock her as she searched up and down the paths for what she sought. She stopped now and then to examine the tongue twister plants that Ms. Blue Fairygodmother had put on display, covering as much ground as she could. An hour later, she found what she was looking for, near the amphitheater and stowed it in her black bag. That witch would see who had the last laugh now. Rapunzel only hoped it would be her and her friends!

Since Snow was busy spying on her stepmom, Cinda, Rapunzel, and Red spent the rest of the morning and early afternoon tending to the events they were in charge of as well as Snow's. Later, when the three girls were sitting together munching Gloomburgers and Doomdogs near Mistress Hagscorch's gazebo, Snow's disembodied voice spoke, nearly giving all three of them heart attacks.

"You'll never guess what!" she whispered. "The E.V.I.L. Society meeting is in half an hour. And it's in the witch's tower!" Snow took off her tiara, revealing herself to them.

"If only we could get up there somehow, we could hide and then listen in," suggested Cinda.

"I think I can get in by using one of the witch's chants," Rapunzel said slowly. "But only because the tower knows me. It won't let you guys up." She didn't mention that there was a good chance she wouldn't be able to get *out* of the tower once inside, though. The tower's magic would probably try to keep her there, just as it had when she was little. But that was a chance she'd have to take. There was too much at stake for her *not* to.

Just before sunset, Rapunzel's BFFs stood back and watched her touch a certain stone near the base of the tower. As the stone warmed under her hand, she chanted:

Tower wall of granite stone,
Open up this door unshown.

Creak! A small door appeared, opened, and admitted her to the tower. From experience, she knew the stairs beyond the door led upward, but they would disappear behind her as she took them, making it impossible to come back down.

Once inside, she turned to wave good-bye to her friends. "Well —" she started to say. *Slam!* The door flew shut in their surprised faces, sealing Rapunzel inside and keeping them out. The only way to go now was up.

The stairs were winding and dark. After taking a deep breath, she put her foot on the first one. Then the next. She took each step slowly, one by one. Her white-knuckled hands gripped the handrail as she went up, up, up, ascending to heights that were almost as lofty as the Pearl Tower dorms. She'd never ventured this high by stairs before, except with the help of her friends. She stopped now and then, trembling with fright. Then she forced herself to go on, ever upward, motivated by the thought that the very future of Grimmlandia could depend on her getting up these steps. She *had* to make it to the top before the Society did so she could hide and listen in on their meeting to discover their evil plans!

Finally, she stepped into the tower room. The place where she'd grown up but had hoped never to see again. Being here and having climbed all those steps kind of made her feel like throwing up. Still, she'd made it! And she was the first to arrive.

The big star painted on the floor in the center of the circular room was still there. And also her little bed, a wardrobe, her shelves of books, and her desk, where she used to practice her letters. She took it all in in a sweeping glance and shivered, feeling like she'd returned to a prison.

Without showing herself at the window, she picked up a small pebble from the stone floor and tossed it out to let her friends know she'd arrived. There were a few pieces of straw on the floor by the window ledge. Mordred must've left them when the witch captured him up here after the pet show.

Hearing strange voices, she quickly hid in the wardrobe where some of her girlish gowns still hung. Just in the nick of time. The voices were closer now. E.V.I.L. was inside the tower room! She hadn't heard any footsteps coming up the stairs, but somehow, the Society had arrived. From her hiding place, she listened to their meeting begin. The closed wardrobe door muffled their words, so she couldn't tell exactly who was speaking half the time. However, she recognized at least two voices. Those of Ms. Wicked and the witch.

Rapunzel opened the wardrobe door a crack, hoping to learn the identities of the members, which could prove helpful in future. The members sat in a circle around the painted star to call up more magical power. However, she saw to her disappointment that they all wore masks to hide their faces. In the center of their circle sat a large old empty trunk she'd never seen before.

"This meeting of the E.V.I.L. Society is now called to order," Ms. Wicked said in a formal tone, quieting all the small talk. "As you all know, E.V.I.L. began back in the Dark Ages, when —" *Oomph!*

The witch elbowed her aside and took over the meeting. "Who cares about all that ancient history? Blah, blah, blah," she said. "What's really important is that, thanks to me, members of E.V.I.L. will soon achieve their rightful place in fairy tales and all of literature. We'll rule the Academy and the realm of Grimmlandia! All because I've collected the rest of the artifacts we need."

She opened her bag and poured the artifacts she'd stolen into the trunk. In went the queen chess piece, toy rabbit, cockleshells, tiara, umbrella, violin, pocket watch, yarn, and zebra. *Q, R, S, T, U, V, W, Y, Z.*

Rapunzel pressed her lips together to keep from gasping. She and her friends had only been guessing before, but now she'd heard it from their own lips. E.V.I.L. hoped to take over the entire realm and everything in it!

Cheers erupted, and clapping. The masked faces all turned toward a big oval, gold-framed mirror that hung on the tower wall. It hadn't been there when Rapunzel first arrived, so she figured Ms. Wicked must have brought it with her. According to Snow, there were hundreds of such fancy, creepy mirrors on the walls of her stepmom's apartment at GA.

A hopeful, waiting excitement filled the tower room as the Society members continued to gaze at the mirror for several long minutes. Suddenly, artifacts began to pour into the room via the mirror, tumbling one by one, then two by two. Into the trunk they went until it was overflowing. These must be the artifacts *A* to *P* that had been listed on the cards in the Grimm brothers' room of the library, she realized. Including Peter Peter's pumpkin and Jack and Jill's pail. Since she knew they'd gone over the wall, that must mean this mirror was somehow connected to the Dark Nothingterror! And it was bringing the artifacts back over the wall. Eventually, the stream of artifacts slowed and then stopped altogether.

Now a mist appeared in the mirror, clouding it. Rapunzel had to press her lips tightly together so she wouldn't gasp or scream when a nose poked out of the misty mirror. Then an eyeball and most of a face appeared. Ludwig! His hands grasped the edges of the mirror as if he would pull himself forward and leap out of it into the room at any moment. How she wished her Grimm girl friends were here with her so she wouldn't be so scared.

But then his image in the mirror began to waver. A surprised look came over his face just seconds before he suddenly vanished!

"What happened? Ludwig? Come back," the witch wailed. She rubbed the ring she wore with the bony fingers of her opposite hand. Ludwig's fingers had been bare, Rapunzel recalled. So she and her friends were probably right that this was his ring. The witch's hat flew off her head as she whirled around and around, flying into a rage as wild as any Principal Rumpelstiltskin might've thrown. "It should have worked. Why didn't it work?" she repeated again and again.

"You've failed!" Ms. Wicked crowed happily. "But no matter. Because I have discovered . . ." She paused, building suspense in her listeners. ". . . the mapestry!" she finished, whipping out the fake mapestry Snow had stitched to show them. According to Snow, her stepmother had been keeping it a secret from the Society, hoping to steal any treasure she found for herself. If she was willing to reveal it now, she must be desperate to make the others think she was more powerful than the witch.

Gathering up every ounce of courage she possessed, Rapunzel flung open the wardrobe doors as dramatically as Red might have done. "I'll tell you why the artifacts didn't work," she announced. Gasps sounded and all heads whipped her way. "Because you have two *P* artifacts . . . but no *X*," she went on. "As in the *xylophone* from the Grimm brothers' room in the library."

And with that, she pulled an object from her bag.

Seeing the xylophone, the witch took a step toward her. "Give me that!" she screamed.

Rapunzel set the xylophone on the floor and poised her foot to stomp it. "If anyone comes nearer — *Crrrunch!* I'll crush this thing under the heel of my boot till it's so out of tune, it won't be of any use to you."

"Wait!" said Ms. Wicked, looking worried. "Surely we can make some deal. What do you want?" She stared into Rapunzel's eyes. Then, as if she'd somehow seen the answer there, she said softly, "What if we could change your fairy tale so your parents never died?"

"What do you mean?" Rapunzel demanded, her attention caught in spite of herself.

"When we — that is, Ludwig — rewrites the great books of Grimm, we could get him to say your parents didn't die. They could come alive in the new version of the story and join E.V.I.L. You could join us, too," said Snow's stepmom.

"Listen to her," coaxed the witch, her competition with Ms. Wicked momentarily shoved aside. When Rapunzel stared at her uncertainly, the witch asked, "Shall I tell you the real reason your mother and father made their bargain with me? It was because I told them what rampion could do."

"Give them their hearts' desire," the other Society members chanted softly.

The witch nodded. "And do you know what your parents desired above all else?"

Rapunzel shook her head, almost afraid to hear.

"A child to love. You!" the witch crooned. She whipped Rapunzel's comb from her bag — the comb she'd stolen back. "See the bellflower design along the comb's edge? That's rampion — another word for Rapunzel. That's why they made the bargain. They hoped to go back on it when I came for you, but naturally I prevailed."

"Just imagine if you could hug them right now," Ms. Wicked chimed in. "Talk to them, too."

Sweet tears of happiness filled Rapunzel eyes as she gazed at the comb, imagining just that.

"All you have to do is give us that last artifact," promised the witch. "And it will come to pass. We'll make sure of it."

All these years Rapunzel had tried to steel herself against her parents for their poor bargain, but now it turned out they'd loved her. They'd yearned for a child — her — which meant they'd *really* loved her. What wouldn't she give to see and talk to them! And that would also mean that she would never have to go live with the witch again!

But then her heart twisted inside her chest. According to the deal she was being offered, her parents would be expected to join the Society. As would she. They'd all become evil, and she'd have only herself to blame for it.

Still, she carefully considered the matter, not wanting to make another bad bargain. "No," she said at last, shaking her head slowly. She couldn't switch sides and work against her friends and all the good people of Grimmlandia! "I won't agree."

The witch and Ms. Wicked both looked taken aback by her answer.

Sensing that it would go better for her if she flattered the witch and made her feel more important than Ms. Wicked, Rapunzel turned and spoke directly to her. "But I *will* make a different deal, only with you."

At this, the witch smiled triumphantly, while Ms. Wicked glowered.

"I'll give you this xylophone in exchange for the onyx comb," Rapunzel continued. "But you must first swear — on Ludwig's ring — that neither you nor any of the members of E.V.I.L. will ever try to steal another artifact again."

Though Ms. Wicked pouted, she, the witch, and the other Society members consulted one another, murmuring together in a huddle.

"Agreed," the witch said finally, holding the comb out to Rapunzel. She was grinning from ear to ear, obviously thinking she'd pulled off another grand bargain.

"One more thing," Rapunzel added, not yet reaching for the comb. "Before you give it to me, I want you to remove any spells you've put on my charm to make it obey you, so I'm certain you can't steal it again. And I make A's in Bespellings class, so don't try to trick me. I won't fall for it like I did the last time."

The witch nodded. Eager to get on with their deal, she quickly recited a spell:

Rapunzel's charm you are.
Rapunzel's charm you'll be.
Work your magic only for her,
And never return to me.

Even though she was overjoyed, Rapunzel tried not to show it as she took the comb. She handed over the xylophone to the witch, who tossed it into the trunk with the other artifacts. Then the Society members turned to look at the mirror again.

"Leader? Are you there?" Ms. Wicked whispered.

"What's wrong, Ludwig?" the witch demanded when nothing happened. "Do you need your ring?" She took off his gold ring and tossed it at the mirror. It disappeared through the center of the mirror, taking with it the last bit of mist that remained. Then the mirror turned completely flat and reflective again. There was no sign of Ludwig at all. Not even the tip of his prominent nose showed through. "Why didn't it work?" wailed the witch.

"Because my friends and I have tricked you," Rapunzel announced. The members' attention swiveled toward her as she pointed to the xylophone that lay atop the heap of artifacts in the trunk. "That xylophone is actually a toy, not a library artifact. I grew it on a tongue twister plant in Bespellings class last week. And an hour ago, I picked it from that very plant, which is now on the festival grounds with even more xylophones growing on it."

"You dare to trick me?" The witch snarled in stunned disbelief. "Deal's off. We'll take that comb and the artifacts and you may stay here alone forever to contemplate your treachery!"

But as she was ranting, Rapunzel was whispering to her comb. If it truly was her charm, it would do what she needed it to. And it did! Instantly, it grew wider and taller, its teeth stretching, bending, and crisscrossing as it formed a cage around the trunk of artifacts to protect them from the Society's clutches.

"Our plan is ruined!" one of the members groaned. Then he suddenly leaped from the floor and into the mirror, disappearing from the room. The others began to follow, leaving the tower by way of the magical mirror, one by one. So that was how they'd all gotten into the tower! Ms. Wicked was the last to go, taking the mirror with her as she leaped through it. Now only Rapunzel and the witch were left in the high tower room.

"You think you've won?" the witch sneered. "Not so! Each of the artifacts we stole has already done harm to the wall around Grimmlandia. Your actions may have prevented Ludwig from traveling here for now, but we've succeeded in making certain . . . loopholes . . . in the fairy tales, nursery rhymes, and other literature as well. Story holes through which he and other Society members will be able to travel on occasion to rewrite the tales. Even without the artifacts, we now have more power than ever before. And we'll get what we want in the end. Remember, evil is the new good." She let out a long, horrifying cackle, displaying her pointy, pea-green teeth.

Rapunzel began backing away from her, moving toward the safety of the wardrobe. Before she made it there, however, the witch whispered, "Rapunzel, Rapunzel, let down your hair!"

Then, just as had happened when Rapunzel was a little girl, her glossy black hair pulled her to the window, where it whipped outside, growing longer and longer until its ends touched the ground below. Since Ms. Wicked had taken the mirror with her, the witch needed some other getaway and was resorting to her tried and true method of departure.

After leaping from the window, the witch began to climb down Rapunzel's long hair. Fortunately, Rapunzel and her friends had anticipated that something like this might happen. But would their plan to capture the witch work?

Peering down, she could see the other three Grimm girls standing at the ready below. Red had opened her basket and was setting the book of Grimm Fairy Tales they'd brought from the *G* section of the library to lie open on the ground at the tower's base. Quickly, Rapunzel pulled a new object from her black bag — a pair of silver scissors. Without giving herself time to change her mind, she began to cut her hair to shoulder length. *Snip! Snip! Snip!* The cut hair tumbled from the window, catching the witch off guard.

"Nooo!" she heard the witch wail. Still battling her fear of heights, Rapunzel held onto the window ledge tightly and watched the would-be Wonderful Witch Twitch tumble down, down, down.

She landed smack-dab in the middle of a page in the Grimm Fairy Tales book Red had set upon the ground as part of their plan. It lay open to an illustration of the tower in Rapunzel's fairy tale!

When the witch hit the open book, there was a whooshing sound as she turned into a plume of pea-green smoke. The smoke whirled like a small tornado that became smaller and smaller as it was magically sucked into the page. As the smoke began to clear, the witch appeared beside the tower in the illustration.

"Now!" yelled Cinda as the smoke faded away completely.

"Gotcha!" Snow slammed the book shut before the witch could escape.

"Yes!" Red exclaimed. "According to that spell book we looked at in the library, *Spells to Foil Fairy-Tale Crooks*, if she stays in there for at least a day, she's well and truly trapped." The three Grimm girls did a happy dance. Watching from above, Rapunzel grinned at them.

"How did you get up there? You hate heights," an alarmed boy's voice called up to her. It was Basil! He'd just arrived with Awesome, probably hoping to try again to scale the tower. "We have to get you down."

With a sharp gasp, Rapunzel drew back from the edge of the window, trembling as she recalled how high she was. "And the artifacts, too," she called back. "All the missing ones are in here with me."

Although she was too far from the window now to see those standing below it, she heard much murmuring and discussion. A few more voices joined the others, including Prince Perfect's.

Oh, perfect, she thought. *Not.* She and her friends hadn't thought through this part of their plan very well and she really didn't want him to see her in this potentially grimmbarrassing predicament. Her hair would soon grow longer, of course. But she couldn't very well climb down her own hair. She had no way out of the tower unless the witch let her out. And the witch was gone.

Just then, they all heard someone shout, "The gazebos are on fire!"

12

Over by the snack area, flames flashed high. Had those three cooks finally started an all-out war? Rapunzel worried. Then she remembered she had the power to help. Quickly, she shrank the comb charm to regular size and tossed it onto the bed so she could grab Jack and Jill's pail from the artifact trunk. When in the twins' hands, the pail could magically resize itself to hold great quantities of water.

"Look out below!" she yelled, tossing the pail out the window. Basil caught it and took off with it along with some of his friends, all running toward the food gazebos. Then she backed away from the window again. A few minutes later, in the distance she saw them pass the pail to Jack and Jill, who filled it with water from the Once Upon River and quickly put out the flames.

"Rapunzel," Red called up. "I just checked the X on the *You Know What*, and guess what? It's showing that we are in the exact right spot. I think what we've been looking for is in the tower somewhere!"

"Okay, I'm on it!" Rapunzel called down. Excited now and glad to have something else to think about besides being trapped so high, she moved away from the window and began searching the room. What kind of treasure would she find? Gold and jewels as Snow had often hoped? She peeked under the bed in the old trunk, and in the wardrobe. Nothing. As she hunted for treasure, the three girls below called out "warm" or "cool," depending on how the golden thread indicator on the mapestry reacted to the places Rapunzel moved.

"Very warm!" Snow called at last.

Rapunzel was back at the wall now, only two feet from the window. She picked up the closest object — a candlestick on a side table. When her BFFs didn't call out, she kept moving in a small circle, picking up other things.

"Red hot!" called Red a few seconds later.

Rapunzel was standing right in front of the window now. She looked up. She looked down. She glanced around. But she saw no treasure. She got on her hands and knees. Maybe there was a loose stone and the treasure was under it? She brushed away the pieces of straw Mordred had left and dug at the edges of the stones with her fingers, but she couldn't pry the stones loose. She sat back. A piece of the straw had gotten caught in the hem of her skirt, so she pulled it out. Instantly, an ancient, disembodied voice spoke:

This straw of old

Can spin into gold.

"The *X* just disappeared from the *You Know What!*" called Snow. "Do you have . . . *It*?" The treasure, she meant.

Rapunzel stared at the straw she held between thumb and forefinger. It certainly didn't look like treasure to her. But what about that spooky voice?

Hearing another odd sound, she jumped to her feet and looked out the window to see Principal R marching a group of knights in armor across the island in her direction. *Clink, clank, clink.* Prince, Perfect, Awesome, Wolfgang, and Basil were walking right alongside them.

Rapunzel tucked the single piece of straw into her black bag as the principal arrived and stationed the knights around the base of the tower. "Good work recapturing the artifacts," he called up to her as she lowered them down from the tower window a few at a time on a makeshift sling of tied-together bedsheets. Briefly, she considered the possibility of escaping the tower in the bedsheet sling herself. But the idea of descending the heights that way was so terrifying that she got dizzy just thinking about it. No way. Climbing up the tower stairs had been hard enough!

After what she'd just witnessed in the tower room, it no longer seemed wise to keep E.V.I.L. a secret as she and her

BFFs had done in the past. Everyone needed to know what that rotten society had planned, in order to be on guard against them.

"The E.V.I.L. Society was just here," Rapunzel announced to one and all. "And they had a magic mirror. They were trying to use it to transport their leader from the Dark Nothingterror into Grimmlandia!" She left it to Red, Snow, and Cinda to answer the questions that were sure to follow her statements.

As she continued to methodically lower artifacts, she heard snatches of what her friends and the others down on the ground were saying. "It's a tricky situation, all right," she heard the principal say. "But the evil characters have a right to exist in the tales, too. Though I admit, it's a balancing act to keep them from trying to up their evil hold on matters."

What? Did that mean he'd known about E.V.I.L.'s plans all along? Rapunzel wondered. She and her friends had never been sure. But if he had known, why hadn't he done more to try to stop E.V.I.L.? It seemed a little bit late, showing up now with his group of knights.

Once the artifacts were all safely below, the knights took charge of them and the fairy-tale book Rapunzel had borrowed, and marched off toward the Academy to return everything to the library. Despite his words in defense of E.V.I.L.'s existence, Principal R looked worried about what she'd told them. After again congratulating Rapunzel and the other Grimm girls on retrieving the artifacts, he urged her to come down from the tower.

"Um, not possible," she called, standing back from the window. "The stairs only lead up, not down."

"How about climbing down the bedsheets?" she heard Perfect suggest.

He has to be aware of my great fear of heights, so why would he even suggest that? she thought with sudden annoyance. Did he really know so little about her? If so, why had he even asked her to the ball?

"Are you dense?" Basil asked him. "She doesn't *do* heights." That made her smile. At least Basil got her.

"Perhaps Ms. Goose could fly over and give you a ride out of there?" Principal R suggested. Another less-than-helpful suggestion, given her fears.

It seemed everyone had a rescue idea. Many involved using magic. Like flying her down on a magical kite, or creating a rainbow to slide down, or making a super-tall beanstalk grow next to the tower. While they discussed various options, Rapunzel again considered the bedsheets she'd tied together. She could *not* climb down them without freaking out. It was a preposterous idea. Right?

Still, something made her reel in the sheets and begin to tie more knots along them at intervals to help her get a foothold. When she was finished, she tossed the sheet-rope back out of the tower. She tested the end that she'd tied to a bar beneath the window when she'd made her sling. Good. It was still secure. Her back to the window, she put her hands on the ledge behind her, preparing to heave herself up and over. Then her eyes fell on the comb lying on the bed next to her black bag. She'd almost forgotten her things!

She ran to the bed and picked up the comb. "Wish me luck," she whispered to it. Giving it a quick kiss, she tucked it into her bag, which she slung over one shoulder. As she sat on the window ledge, there were a few gasps from outside, then a hush fell over the group below. Taking a deep breath, she lowered herself down the side of the tower.

Keeping her eyes firmly on the makeshift rope — not the ground — she *slooowly* and carefully moved lower. "Don't look down, don't look down," she murmured to herself over and over along the way. When she reached the base of the tower, she stared at her three best friends, feeling stunned. They stared back at her in amazement.

"I can't believe you did that!" Cinda squealed happily.

"Neither can I," Rapunzel admitted.

"It was a towering triumph!" said Red.

"Yeah," Snow agreed, nodding her head up and down so hard that her tiara tilted sideways.

"I know! And I was hardly scared at all," Rapunzel told them gleefully. "I think my new comb . . . I mean my *charm*, must have the power to calm my fears . . . at least when it comes to heights." When she pulled out the comb charm to show them, the piece of straw came out with it and fell to the ground.

Principal R's eyes lit up when he saw the straw. As he plucked it from the ground, it began to glitter and gleam brightly in the sun. He did a happy little jig. "How grimmensely grimmnificent! You found the legendary treasure. The Straw of Gold! With the right magic, it will make more and more and more." He ran off with it, kicking his heels and shouting. "The Academy is saved at last!"

Rapunzel and the other GA students stared after him.

"So the treasure we've searched for all this time is a piece of straw?" asked Cinda.

"A magical straw that can apparently be turned into gold," Rapunzel corrected.

"I think there's a story about that in the fairy tales somewhere," said Red.

"No jewels, though?" Snow said in disappointment. But then she cheered up. "At least we *found* the treasure."

The four BFFs high-fived, laughing in delight. Since the boys were staring at them in confusion, the girls showed them the mapestry and explained everything, or most of it anyway. As Rapunzel and her three friends began walking toward the snack gazebos, the guys followed, examining the mapestry in fascination.

As her friends were speculating on the cause of the earlier fire, Rapunzel snapped her fingers as she figured something out. "That treasure straw came from some bales of straw I found here on the island and spread on the ground for the pet show. Mordred must've gotten some of it caught in his fur during the judging. When he was captured in the tower by the witch, the magic straw must have fallen from his fur to the floor."

"Just think!" said Cinda in wonderment. "If he hadn't found that exact piece of straw, we'd never have located it ourselves. It would've been like looking for a needle in a towering haystack."

"A needle we didn't even know was the treasure," added Red.

Snow nodded. "And that explains why you saw the *X* on the mapestry move to Neverwood Forest for a while yesterday," she told Red. "Because the tower took Mordred there after the pet show and then returned here again with the straw he'd left inside."

As the other girls continued chatting, Perfect called to Rapunzel. She dropped back to walk with him.

"So you cut your hair," he remarked right away, sounding like he disapproved.

"Uh-huh." Slowly, Rapunzel shook her head from side to side. She was used to long hair swishing all the way to her knees. Now it barely brushed her shoulders. This was a fun change, but she still preferred it long. "It'll grow back," she told Perfect. For some reason, she didn't feel so tongue-tied around him anymore. Or so thrilled to be talking to him either. Even though she actually *had* taken his suggestion to climb down the bedsheet in the end, it still rankled that he'd seemed to know so little about her.

"But will it be long again by tonight?" Perfect asked impatiently as they continued walking behind the rest of the group.

"Well, no. By the end of the week, though. My hair grows really fast. It's a curse spell the witch from the tower put on me long ago." Didn't he know that about her either? She knew lots of little details about him. For instance, he liked oatsqueal for breakfast, while Basil liked knick-knack paddy-whack pancakes. If you liked someone as a friend, you paid attention and learned things about them.

"Oh." He shifted his shoulders and looked away. After a minute, he spoke again. "Um, there's something I need to tell you."

Rapunzel lifted an eyebrow. "Yes?"

Squirming a little, he stared down at the ground. "I . . . um . . . I forgot that I had already asked Princess Pea to the Festival Ball before I asked you to go. So . . ."

Rapunzel came to a dead halt and frowned at him. From the way he avoided looking her in the eye, she knew he was lying. Suddenly, she guessed why.

"You're backing out on me because I *cut my hair*?" she asked in shock.

"Huh? No. That would be . . ."

"Shallow?" she supplied. "Superficial?"

He didn't reply, which meant she'd guessed right. That hurt, but on the other hand, did she really want to go to the ball with a boy who didn't have the courage to tell her he'd changed his mind about going with her? If simply cutting her hair had caused him to fall out of like with her, then he was more of a loser than she would've thought possible. And realizing that made him even less appealing.

"Well, thanks for telling me," she said, more politely than he probably deserved. "Have fun."

"Yeah, thanks," he said with relief. "I was afraid you'd get mad. No hard feelings, then?"

Rapunzel shook her head. "Nope. It's okay. But I do wish you'd had the guts to tell me the truth. You should work on that." She had the satisfaction of seeing his jaw drop. She sprinted forward to catch up with her friends, who'd pulled way ahead of the boys by now. When she told them what had happened, they got even madder than she was.

"Why, that skunk!" said Snow.

"No, he's lower than a skunk. More like a worm," said Red.

"The slimy icky kind," added Cinda.

Rapunzel grinned at their idea of support. "Thanks, guys. Anyway, I'll have more fun hanging out with you at the ball." Although her three besties were going with their crushes, she knew that the four of them would likely all wind up hanging out together more than with the guys, as usually happened.

When they reached the snack gazebos, a reporter from the *Grimm News* was interviewing Ms. Queenharts, who was pointing a finger at Ms. Jabberwocky. "She let out a fiery burp and melted all the snacks to smithereens!" the teacher complained.

It seemed that only the rampion ship dessert had survived the fire. Which meant that Mistress Hagscorch won the Best Snack Award by default. However, Rapunzel noted that, to her credit, Hagscorch let the other two snack creators get some of the glory, too. Not only was she letting Ms. Queenharts give all the quotes for the article that would surely be printed in this week's *News*, Ms. Jabberwocky was posing for a *News* photographer.

Bonggg! As night fell, a gong sounded to signal that it was almost time for the Festival Ball. Seeming to have been satisfied by the attention they were getting because of the fire, all three cooks abruptly came together as a team. They rescued what treats they could, taking the least burnt ones and the rampion ship over to the big white tent where the dance would be held.

"Too bad about the ball tonight," called Mary Mary Quite Contrary as she passed the girls on her way to the changing room. "I think it's going to rain."

The girls looked up to see a multitude of stars glittering in a beautiful dark blue sky. Smiles broke out on their faces. There was no rain in sight. Mary Mary was simply being contrary again!

"Things are getting back to normal," Red said, sounding relieved that the girl wasn't acting so weirdly cheerful anymore.

"Must be because the artifacts are back where they belong," said Snow.

"C'mon, let's get moving!" said Cinda. A feeling of excitement swirled around them as they all four zipped over to the temporary changing room where the GA girls' ball gowns had been hung.

As they helped each other dress in their finery, Rapunzel finally revealed the very last secret she'd been keeping from her friends. "I've never told you this before, but my tower task is . . . Gatherer."

With puzzled expressions on their faces, Snow, Cinda, and Red looked at each other and then back at her. "Is that supposed to be a problem?" asked Snow.

"Well, it *is* a task for a witch," Rapunzel replied. "I never told you before because I wasn't sure how you'd feel about that . . ." Her voice trailed off.

Red shrugged. "There are good witches as well as bad witches, right? Wolves, too. Wolfgang used to worry that he was evil just because his uncles were big and bad, but he tries very hard not to be. I figure we all have a choice about which way we go."

Snow and Cinda nodded vigorously.

Rapunzel cocked her head, thinking about what they'd said as she put on the cute ankle-boots she'd chosen for the dance. "Ludwig chose evil," she remarked. Then she smiled. "But if I ever turn into a witch, I think I'll want to be a good one."

"Of course you will," said Cinda matter-of-factly. "No worries on that score!"

Gazing at their reflections in the mirror, Rapunzel heaved a big, happy sigh. "I think I am done with worries. For tonight, anyway."

"Yeah, instead of *worrying*, we should be *hurrying* to that ball!" Red said. They all giggled.

In no time at all, everyone was *scurrying* off for the big white tent. Snow in her pale blue-green satin gown with little blue-green rosettes at the neckline that matched the gems in the tiara she wore. Cinda in her glass slippers and a frothy pink gown with poufy tulle overlaying its full skirt. Red in her white velvet gown with red piping on the sleeves, neckline, and hem. And Rapunzel in her black lacy gown and dressy-heeled ankle boots. Thanks to Snow's urging, the gown had diamond sparkles and she even wore a band of sparkles in her hair.

The inside of the open-air tent was decorated with pink and white heart-shaped balloons and curly streamers that slowly danced around the tent near the ceiling in time to the music. There were small white tables around the edges of the tent, and the musicians were playing at one end. Large bouquets from Mary Mary's garden sat here and there, with smaller bouquets in the center of each table.

To kick off the ball, Principal R gave a short speech. He was smiling big as he began, "First, the bad news. Although the fair was lots of fun, we didn't make enough money to save the school." Disappointed murmurs filled the tent. "Now the good news. What I just told you doesn't matter because the legendary treasure of Grimmlandia has been found. And all the missing artifacts are now properly back in place in the Grimmstone Library!" Wild cheers greeted this news and he had to yell over them to be heard. "More to come on that in morning announcements next week! For now, enjoy the ball!"

Rapunzel and her friends looked at one another, pleased, but also a little doubtful. Though he'd seemed to suggest that all was well, they knew better. Sure, they'd trapped the witch and forced Ludwig back into the Dark Nothingterror . . . for now. But it seemed a certainty that Ms. Wicked and those other mysterious E.V.I.L. Society members would get up to more mischief in the days to come. Their threat to change the endings of fairy tales to benefit E.V.I.L. was still very real, and *dangerous*. Did the principal really think that the evil and good characters in the Grimm tales could happily and peaceably coexist from here on out? Not likely! Rapunzel and her friends would have to remain on guard for the safety of their school and all of Grimmlandia.

Still, tonight they would let their hearts be light. They would enjoy an evening of fun and friendship. As the principal left the podium, the four Grimm girls were the first ones onto the dance floor, whirling and twirling with one another. Soon some of the boys joined them.

There were plenty of guys to dance with. Rapunzel asked Prince Foulsmell to dance first. Perhaps because of his unfortunate name, he was often overlooked. In her opinion, though, he was adorable and sweet. From time to time, she saw Perfect dancing with various girls, all of them among the most beautiful at GA. He was one of the most handsome guys for sure. But he was far from perfect, unless it counted that he was a perfect *twit*. The idea made her smile.

Later in the evening, Principal R awarded Mistress Hagscorch's Rampion Championship prize to all four girls for having saved the school from an evil plot and for finding the treasure. And Rapunzel's tongue twister plant was voted the winning plant for the role it had played in rescuing the artifacts.

"Couldn't have happened to a more deserving student," Mistress Hagscorch told her with a gruff sort of fondness. She handed Rapunzel a silver cake knife and gestured toward the ship-shaped Championship dessert. "Careful now. That thing packs a surprise." Then she backed away.

Rapunzel eyed the big ship dessert warily. Was its frosting going to explode or something? As she sliced into it, she noticed that it was all fluffy inside like cake. And it smelled yummy. It was nothing like spinach!

Then suddenly, as she sliced deeper, the big ship magically split apart into dozens and dozens of small tart-size ships. There was delight on everyone's faces as she and her friends placed the little ships on small plates and passed them out to all. *Good* magic, like Hagscorch's bewitched cookery, was so grimmtabulous!

As everyone crowded around to take a ship, Mistress Hagscorch reminded them, "Don't forget to wish for your hearts' desires."

"So I can make this taste like whatever I desire?" Wolfgang asked, considering his ship. "Like if I said gym socks, that's what it would taste like?"

"Eew!" said Red, giggling. "If that's what your heart

desires, I pity your poor heart. Or maybe I should say, your poor stomach!"

"I think it's more about giving you a taste of something you yearn for or love," said Rapunzel. "Like if you always wanted to be able to sing, you suddenly could, at least as long as your ship lasts."

Cinda took a bite of hers. "Mmm. Bubble gum."

"You wished for bubble-gum-flavored dessert?" Awesome teased her. "*That's* your heart's desire?"

Cinda grinned, nodding. "But I was remembering a bubble-blowing contest I once had with my mom before she died. It was almost like she was here beside me again."

Hearing this, everyone got even more excited. They contemplated what they desired and then took bites of their ship-shaped desserts, telling the others what they felt or saw when their desire was realized. "When I took a bite, I felt like I was swimming in a magical underwater castle!" exclaimed Mermily.

"I had my cockleshells back," said Mary Mary. At which point, Snow reminded her that her shells weren't missing any longer but were safely back in the Grimmstone Library. "Rabsnackle," said Mary Mary. "I should've wished for a garden of pretty maids all in a row instead."

"Can't decide about your heart's desire?" Basil asked, appearing at Rapunzel's side. He pointed to her uneaten ship.

"I already have all my heart desires," she replied. She was thinking especially about her three BFFs and her special comb charm — a charm her parents had made especially for her. Because they'd loved her.

Basil grinned. "Then how about wishing for a dance with me?" he asked.

She grinned at him. "Deal." She squeezed her eyes shut briefly, then popped them open and took a bite of her ship. "Done," she said, setting her ship on a nearby table.

"How about that," Basil said, taking the gloved hand she held out to him. "Your heart's desire matches mine!"

As they swept out onto the dance floor, she tossed her head in an automatic gesture that she used to flip her long hair back. She was startled to remember that her hair was much shorter now. She reached up to touch it, then looked at Basil uncertainly.

"You look nice," he assured her.

"Really?" she said. Almost all the girls at the ball wore fancy, fashionable dresses edged with satin ribbon. Colorful dresses, not black like hers. "You don't think I look like a dead weed among flowers?" she teased. "You don't think my hair is too short?"

"No," he answered. "I think you look like you. Cool. Not afraid to be different. Grimmazing."

She gave a light laugh, not taking him seriously, and angled her head to look up at him. "You know, I think I'm glad I saved you from that bully back in first grade," she teased.

He arched a brow at her. "You didn't *really* save me. I only pretended to be scared of Jack Horner that day."

"What? Why?"

"To get your attention," he said. Then he grinned. "Hey — I was just a kid. I didn't know what else to do to make you notice me. But I knew I liked you the first time I saw you." He looked away for a minute. When he looked back, she saw that his cheeks had flushed a little. "Still do," he admitted.

As the music began to slow and then stop, they stepped apart. Rapunzel stared at him. Because she'd just realized something truly grimmtastic. She liked Basil! As in *like*-liked him.

"Me, too," she told him in a soft voice.

Another song began. Rapunzel looked at him uncertainly and he looked back at her. At the same time, they both blurted, "Want to dance again?"

"Yes!" they answered at the same time. Then they laughed together. And Basil twirled her off to dance the night away among their friends.

Saving the school. Capturing the witch. Finding treasure. Getting her charm. Learning that her parents loved her. And hanging out with her BFFs. In spite of E.V.I.L., this had been one of the very best days of Rapunzel's entire life. And that was the dilly dilly truth!